Blind Spot
They didn't see it coming

Sue Miller

Sue Miller is married with two children and a grandson. She was born in London but after a happy interlude as a student in Leeds has lived most of her life in the north east of England. For many years she held various roles as a teacher, psychologist and senior manager developing and delivering services for children and families. She has always worked in areas where individuals experience the challenging social, economic and environmental pressures that successive governments, as well as communities, try to address. As a university lecturer, Sue published books and articles on parenting, childhood, care and education and the complex leadership and learning issues involved in managing and adapting to change.

Blind Spot is a prequel to her first novel *20/20 Vision: They didn't see it coming*

To Keith

Who has listened and believed in me every single day.

Blind Spot
They didn't see it coming

We learn what we live. What happens 'off camera' in families and communities is arguably as important as the 'centre stage' events.

The tension between how we're *brought up* and how we *turn out* is one that has occupied me all of my life. The way individuals share with and care for the most vulnerable in society often reflects those childhood experiences.

I've come to the conclusion that, whatever else we do, it's important to communicate to our children a simple truth: every human being matters. Whoever we are, wherever we live, we all need to feel we are loved, safe, to know we are accepted and have someone and somewhere to turn. So many children do not know those precious truths.

This story is intended as a prequel to my novel *20/20 Vision*. While I have been writing I've thought a lot about how we cannot avoid juggling what's fair and what's right. Yet whenever I see random acts of kindness my faith in our shared humanity is restored.

The demonstration of trust and compassion towards friends and strangers gives me hope; the courage to face each day's new challenge and to whisper: *Bring it on.*

For Seve

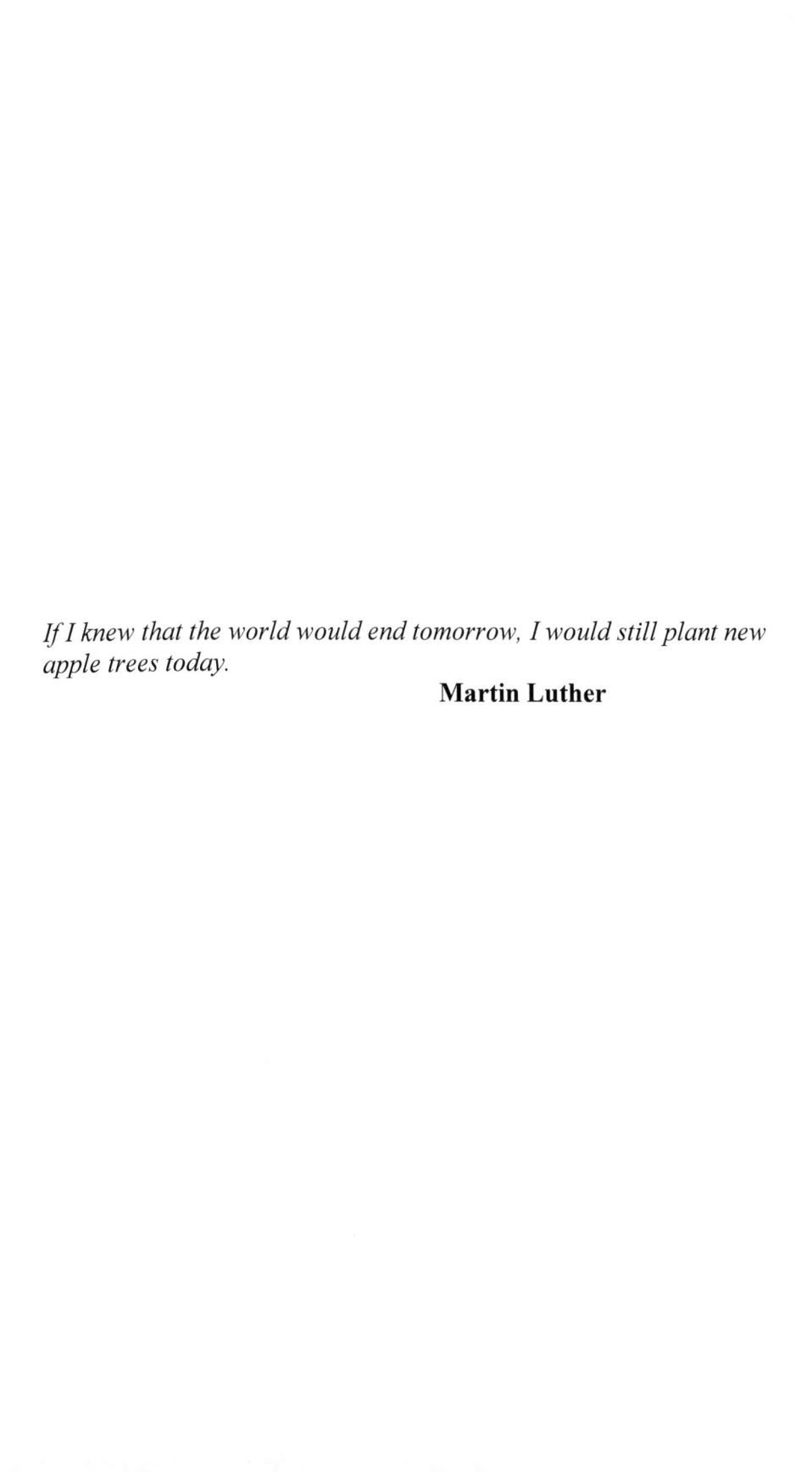

If I knew that the world would end tomorrow, I would still plant new apple trees today.
Martin Luther

2083 Journey's End
September 16th 2083

2045 Thirty Eight Years Earlier
April 7th 2045

2050 Five Years Later
July 17th 2050
July 5th 2051

2054 Three Years Later
September 30th 2054
October 1st 2054
October 5th 2054
October 6th 2054
October 7th 2054
December 2054
December 24th 2054

2060 Six Years Later
October 31st 2060
November 1st 2060
November 5th 2060
June 1st 2061
June 24th 2061
June 25th 2061
July 21st 2061

2061 Correspondence

2083 Twenty Two Years Later
September 17th 2083
September 18th 2083
December 2084
February 15th 2085
March 2085
August 2085
October 1st 2085
October 2nd 2085
December 24th 2085
December 2085
June 2086

2088 Two Years Later
August 2088
August 2089

2095 Six Years later: 'My Story' by Lucy Daniel

2083
Journey's End

The Bay by a Lighthouse
September 16th 2083

Eli felt someone had flicked a switch and he'd been shaken awake. Stopping dead in his tracks, he was overwhelmed by a tsunami of foreboding. His strong, lean body tensed. It was as if a genie had escaped from a bottle.

He focused on the sound. A rhythmic crashing of millions of tons of ocean, salt and sea creatures crushed into tiny pieces of detritus. The sea had been a slumbering giant, chest rising and falling. They had known for years that it was not always benevolent. Drop by icy drop, floe by melted snowy floe it could become an awakening monster, unpredictable and ravenous.

The slap of cold breath on his face was only too familiar, a spray of tangy droplets impregnated with the pungent smell of seaweed. He turned towards the horizon to take in the view, gripping the handle of his fishing rod, feeling its smoothness on his skin.

His wide dark eyes darted across the scene, searching for signs, portents, resting on clouds building on the horizon, as usual; seagulls dipping and gliding seeking a last meal before bedtime, as usual; the impenetrable greyness of a glowering evening sky promising storms to come, as usual.

Nothing was different. But for some reason he felt afraid and fear made him shiver.

As the family's sentinel he had honed his survival instincts, born in part from a life lived always at the margins and handed down from generations of Cassandra-like ancestors. His family had lost count of the times they had averted disaster by listening to Eli's premonitions. He was their prophet.

Although he could distinguish nothing untoward in the darkness, Eli trusted his instincts and took up a position where he could see before being seen. He would fish. That was, after all, why he was here.

Ignoring the chill in the air from the gathering storm, he forced himself to settle to the task. It was evident from the easy flow of his swift movements that he was a seasoned hunter. Within an hour he had baited and cast a dozen times and managed three landings - all coley. It was a good haul considering, even though he had no competition. In the old days there'd have been a whole community of anglers at the shoreline. He smiled down at the catch. It felt good to provide for your family.

Shouldering the bucket and bag and holding his rod like a spear, he turned and strode back up the shingle, leaving the bay and heading towards the causeway and the lighthouse that was home, dipping his head against the wind and driving rain. Stinging his face, it dripped down his neck, finding its way inside the upturned collar of his heavy woollen jacket and, not for the first time, he longed for his old oilskins.

The path snaked towards rocks, stretching out above the waves. He could see the tide was turning and, remembering the earlier unease, increased his pace.

The attack was over in seconds. Eli had no chance even to shout. The sea's voice drowned out the men's footsteps. Stars were shrouded by thick clouds scudding across a brooding skyline. As he was about to turn onto the path they came from behind rocks, sledge hammering into him just before the step up from the beach onto the causeway.

Falling forward onto the knife, his blood flowed into the rising sea. The assailants gathered up his fish and disappeared into the shadows. As his breathing slowed, he managed to lift himself away from the tide line. He needed to be found.

It wasn't supposed to end like this.

Thirty Eight Years Earlier

A Coastal Village
April 7th 2045

'OK, we'll wrap it up there for today. Enjoy your weekend and see you all first thing Monday.'

Nick Grigori flipped the lid down on his laptop and gathered up bundles of papers. The dozen or so others in the room shut down their computers, shrugged on jackets. There were last minute exchanges and finally a hubbub of goodbyes. In a few minutes only two men were left.

'Good meeting,' said Isaac.

Flicking off the light, Nick pulled the door shut, slid the bolts and turned the key in the heavy padlock. He and Isaac made their way down to a headland in front of an old church, falling into a companionable silence.

Stretching away into the distance, bathed in a glorious early evening light, was the sea, clear and blue-grey, dipped in silver. The only sound was the regular swoosh of its waves caressing the shore.

Reaching a row of terraced houses they paused, absorbing the peace.

'Yeah, we're getting there,' said Nick, perching on a dry stone wall bordering a garden. 'Those ideas of making the Programme's front screen a pick and mix patchwork really works. Keeps the user's options open. Makes everyone's journey through the content different.'

'Still got a lot to do on the overseas networking though. Need Paul to put more pressure on their ministers. Does my head in how slow they are.'

Nick grinned. 'Relax, Isaac. Don't be so hard on them. They've got a lot on their plates just now.'

Isaac shrugged and kicked at the wall. 'You'd like to think these people could show a bit of leadership though wouldn't you? We haven't got time to mess about.'

Nick put an arm round his friend's shoulders and, pushing open a gate, steered him up the path towards the front door. It opened and Nick's wife, Eva, long russet hair framing her face and dressed in a loose jumper and beaded skirt speaking more of colour than coordination, waved them in before following the men through to the kitchen. Nick planted a kiss on the top of her head as he and Isaac passed.

'You need a beer mate. It's Friday. Let's get this weekend started.'

He pulled a couple of bottles from a fridge, levered off the tops and handed one to Isaac.

'Home brew. See what you think.'

They chinked bottles and took a long swig. Nick savoured the moment, licking his lips.

'Not bad, not bad at all.'

Activity was everywhere. Vegetables and a couple of plucked chickens were being turned into an evening meal. Eva had joined Isaac's wife Ellie and a boy and girl who looked about ten, all working together, chatting and joking. The children, who were cousins, took carrots and potatoes outside to wash off the rich soil before settling down with bowls at the table to scrape them clean.

Ellie was making pastry. She lifted her floury hands to Isaac's face as she pulled her husband towards her to deposit a kiss. The boy looked across and giggled.

'Dad! You're all floury!'

Pulling away, Isaac glanced across at his reflection in a driftwood framed mirror hanging above the table. He grabbed a cloth and rubbed the powdery dust off his face, dropped the towel, collected his beer and stalked outside. Ellie rolled her eyes and the children smirked at each other.

Eva was in the act of tying her hair back with a ribbon, caught the look and laughed. 'No sense of humour that brother of mine!'

The women layered a large earthenware casserole dish with meat sliced from the chicken carcasses; vegetables lifted steaming from a bubbling pan and handfuls of fresh chopped herbs. Ellie blanketed the mixture with pastry, sealing and crimping the edges. The boy cut out pastry petals which the girl scattered in a beanstalk design across the crust.

'That looks great,' beamed Eva. 'Which of you wants to brush the egg on, Hope or Jude?'

'Me, me!' both children shouted.

'Thought so, there you go. Right into the edges mind.'

Once finished, the pie was transferred with great care to the oven. Eva checked the clock.

'Now go and do your homework. Dinner'll be in about an hour.'

Hope groaned. 'Oh Mum, do we have to? Can't we play out for a bit?'

'No love, you need to get your work done first. You've got all weekend to play.'

Jude had already pulled books from a bag under the table and was settling down to what looked like Maths. Eva smiled across at him.

'See, Hope, Jude's got the right idea. No fuss, he just gets on with it. You could learn from your cousin, my girl.'

Hope poked her tongue out at Jude who was trying not to laugh and with a sigh she also opened an exercise book and took out a pencil.

'I've got English. *'Write a story about Someone Special'*. They give us this every year.

'So who you going to write about?'

'Same person I always do-Baby Mia.'

Jude was busy working on sums. The two mothers exchanged a glance and Ellie came and sat with her niece at the table.

'That's lovely you want to write about mine and your dad's little sister. Need any help?'

Sensing an opportunity to talk rather than write, Hope put down her pen, rested her chin in her hand and gazed wide eyed up into the woman's face.

'What was Mia like Auntie Ellie?'

Ellie sighed. 'Well, certainly special. She was funny and clever and cheeky and we loved her to pieces. Course, your dad was your age when she was born and I was only five so he remembers her more than me, but I'll never ever forget her. I know your Grandpa and Grandma and the doctors did everything they could, but no one really knew what was wrong with her and by the time they did find out she was very poorly. Maybe if she'd been born a bit sooner she'd have been OK. But by the time she got ill there weren't enough medicines to go round to make her better.'

'That's not fair.'

'No darling, it's not. But it's how it was. It still is.'

The room fell silent and Hope, seeming to realise she wasn't going to get any more from her aunt, joined Jude in settling to their respective tasks. Seizing the moment, Eva poured two glasses of wine and the women drifted outside into the fresh early evening air. Nick was leaning over the wall, watching the sunset. Isaac meanwhile paced up and down. The talk was still of the Programme.

'I'm worried we're not going to get finished in time. It feels like internet sites are getting more restricted every day,' said Isaac.

'Governments are trying to get a handle on what's being shared. It's their fault we're in this mess; they have to at least take some responsibility to sort it. There are dangerous people out there.

The last thing politicians will want is for some criminal underclass to start to spread even more lies about what's been going on. The blame gamers will have a field day and heaven knows who'll be scapegoated.'

'Yeah, but trying to licence social media wasn't the answer. People still say what they like, the worst stuff just goes underground and simmers away till something triggers an eruption and it explodes. There'll be an epidemic of hatred, violence fed by the sort of mindless prejudice that always goes sweeping through communities when people feel threatened. We'll have no way of knowing what we're dealing with.'

Isaac swiped at the grass with a cane in frustration 'Bloody do gooders! They should have seen this coming. People have been trolling and abusing the internet since we were kids. It's not like we haven't know for decades the impact of social media on public opinion.'

Ellie tried to put her arms round her husband but he shrugged her off. Nick cocked an eyebrow at Eva.

'It's frustrating, Isaac, I know it is. I'd give anything to be able to turn back the clock, we all would. But it's too late. We have to focus on the Programme now. Whatever happens, at least we'll have tried to do something.'

The words were intended to be reassuring, but they could all see that Isaac wasn't convinced.

'Shall we eat outside tonight? It's plenty warm enough. I've got candles.'

Nick smiled at Eva. His wife always knew how to calm things down. Ellie was standing watching Isaac. She looked downcast. Nick was troubled for his sister. Not for the first time he felt uneasy at his part in having encouraged the relationship between them. The two men had first met as students when Nick found Isaac radical, challenging of the status quo and not afraid to ask difficult, unsettling questions.

Isaac had introduced Nick to his sister Eva. Nick hadn't been particularly looking for a relationship but Eva was too special for him to ignore. She was younger than her brother, funny and caring, generous and warm. It was love at first sight. She and Nick were soul mates.

Hope came to the back door. 'Mum, I think dinner's nearly ready,' she called. 'And Gran and Gramps have arrived. Do you want me and Jude to lay the table?'

'Thanks love.'

All four adults stepped forward to exchange warm hugs with Nick and Ellie's parents, Abe and Sarai. Soon the three generations were sat together, candles glowing in the gathering dusk, each digging in to steaming pie and warm bread, fresh from the oven. Hope had gathered flowers from the garden - a hotchpotch of yellow, white and green, tumbling from a blue jug, petals and pollen scattering onto the table. Abe and Sarai concentrated on the men's tales of the Project, their respect and interest, reassurance and encouragement appearing to act as a salve to Isaac's mood.

As the evening wore on the wine flowed and they all became relaxed and animated. Jude and Hope took turns to present their grandparents with what they were doing at school, glowing in the praise and love they were shown, though they were each so different.

Eva pulled out her phone and captured the moment, later posting it on her timeline. She often recorded ordinary incidents like this. It might just be a family meal, but she knew enough from talking to friends that the quality of the relationship between these three such different generations was very special. She sighed, feeling lucky to have this story to celebrate. Not everyone was as fortunate.

******   ******   ******

They all helped to wash up and then settled down indoors, snuggling into the ancient oversized leather sofa and armchairs that filled the sitting room. The evening air chilled as the sun set but Nick had remembered to light logs in the inglenook fireplace and the room was cosy. Jude and Hope lay in front of the fire, Eva snuggled in Nick's lap, Ellie sitting at Isaac's feet, resting her head on his knees.

The evening news showed the impact of a widespread drought across Africa and the commentator was giving his report.

'Climate changes have, as we know, led to massive shortages in different parts of the African sub continent. Thousands find themselves without some of life's essentials: fertile land, water, food, medicines. Where we visited the situations were particularly serious. On the ground there appears to be a growing combination of chaotic desperation and hopelessness. Representatives from different governments are attempting to deal with an unending tide of human suffering flowing towards ports and borders as families leave their homes to try to find shelter and safety. While sometimes I sensed that locals had come to accept the inevitability of their fate, this was by no means always the case. We saw angry clashes, mass burials and makeshift hospitals. And aid agencies overwhelmed by the levels of need.'

The tear stained face of a young woman cradling her baby son, his eyes huge and staring, skin crawling with flies, was one image Eva found too unbearable to look at.

From the pictures it did appear as if violence was most prevalent at borders. The potential for salvation that a possible crossing into a country perceived as having more resources appeared to spur a final, though often fruitless, fight in refugees. Body bags lined quaysides and road blocks.

The news report ended and Nick turned off the screen. Everyone was quiet.

Sarai reached out to Hope and Jude. 'Come give me hugs you two.'

Hope wrapped her arms round her grandmother who rocked her, smoothing her hair. Jude stayed where he was, staring at the blank screen.

Isaac broke the silence.

'Thank God we've got control of our borders.'

Hope felt her grandmother's arms go rigid. Everyone's eyes turned towards her uncle.

It was Abe that spoke.

'Why son? So we can get help to where it's needed?'

'No, so we can stem the flood. You saw the numbers. If we still had freedom of movement at the borders we'd be over run in days.'

Ellie's head was down. Nick sensed Eva wouldn't be able to keep quiet for long.

'Kids, bed time I reckon. Come on, get your stuff together, say goodnight to everyone. We're all tired.'

There was something in his tone which meant that, for once, Hope didn't argue. She hugged everyone except her Uncle Isaac, who stayed where he was, slumped in the armchair. Ellie and Jude collected up possessions and made for the front door. Nick touched Isaac's arm as he went to pass by and drew him back into the room.

'Mate, there's no call for that sort of talk. Not in front of the kids. You of all people know why it matters that we keep borders open.'

Isaac shrugged off Nick's restraining arm. He was the shorter of the two and in the firelight his upturned face was flushed with a combination of home brew and raw emotion.

'This is what I've been trying to talk to you about all evening, Nick. It's the people at the top. We've been telling them for years how climate change would impact on resources. They've taken no notice and now they're wringing their hands pretending to care. It's too late! They should have acted while they had the chance, made people pay attention and not keep making out a few of us are entitled to take what we want and sod the rest. Now we've got this mess and one day our kids are going to have to deal with it because we didn't.'

Grabbing his work bag, Isaac strode out and slammed the front door as he left. Abe and Sarai came back into the room.

'Did you speak to him?'

'I did. He's upset.'

Eva started to gather up glasses. 'He's upset! What about the rest of us?'

Nick sighed. 'He's got a point you know. Everyone's known this was coming.'

'I know, but we can't turn back the clock. And if he has a point, that's not the way to show it. The kids get enough of that sort of talk at school and on the internet. They don't need it from someone they're meant to look up to.'

She hugged Abe and Sarai and turned towards the stairs. 'Sorry guys, it's been a long day, do you mind if I hit the sack?'

'Course not, love. We'll get going too. It's been a lovely evening. Thanks for dinner.'

Nick walked his parents to the door and held his mother's coat for her to shrug into.

'I'm worried about Ellie,' she said. 'She's lost her sparkle.'

'I know Mum. I'll talk to Isaac. He's under a lot of pressure. He wants the Programme to work every bit as much as the rest of us do.'

'You're all under pressure, just some of you seem to handle it better than others,' muttered Sarai. 'I never liked him.'

'Now Mum, come on. Don't be like that. I'll speak to him.'

Abe hugged his son and taking Sarai's hand the two strolled down the path. Nick watched them till they disappeared round the corner towards the headland to the tiny fisherman's cottage they called home. He rested his head against the door frame, looking up at a myriad stars that appeared close enough to touch. There was no cloud blanket and he felt a chill in the air. Sighing, he braced himself for what he suspected Eva would be waiting to say about her brother. He knew what his mum meant about Ellie though, she wasn't herself and he didn't like seeing that either.

Snuffing out the candles, he stood a fireguard in front of the glowing embers in the grate and started up the stairs.

Bloody families.

Five Years Later

July 17th 2050

'You all ready for tonight?

Nick lifted a slice of toast and crammed it into his mouth.

'This is five years of work we're going to be talking about. If we're not ready now we'll never be.' He grinned up at his wife. 'Five years! Can you believe it?'

The time had flown. Eva had been busy with her work in administration, helping to establish small community initiatives that sparked from ideas that children and parents at the local primary school came up with and doing what she could to support all members of their family as different needs arose. Nick had become absorbed in what was now called the *20/20 Vision Project*. The team had built a strong reputation for delivery. His head of department at the University was a fierce advocate and had managed to manoeuvre some of Nick's teaching commitments and the Department's funding streams to support the work.

'We'd be nowhere without Max's help you know,' Nick had commented to Eva. 'He'll be there tonight, rooting for us. It's a chance to thank him publically.'

The meeting was due to start at 5.30pm. Eva arrived at the Heritage Centre early, but the car park was already full, semi abandoned vehicles perched on grass verges. A van made to turn into the driveway but the driver thought better of it and instead deposited another ten or so people on the roadside.

They were all ages, men, women and children still in school uniforms and babies in push chairs. Eva didn't envy the parents, she remembered only too well those days of manoeuvring Hope as a sleeping toddler through crowds. Resting her shoulder against the glass door, she wove through the melee, signed herself in and headed for the queue for drinks.

Feeling an arm round her shoulder, she looked up. It was Nick.

'Hi love, glad you could make it.'

'You're not exactly short of punters,' she joked nodding round the room. 'The entire village must be here. Got your speech?'

'You bet I have! See you later. I just need to catch up with a couple of people.'

She watched him work his way to the front, greeting friends by name and shaking hands with strangers.

'He's born for this,' she thought to herself, smiling.

Isaac was already on the stage, checking equipment, testing the microphone, looking flustered. Jude emitted tangible teenage awkwardness hovering alongside him, holding a pile of papers. His father turned and saw them. Eva couldn't hear what was said but it was obvious Isaac wasn't happy. Jude blushed and scurried off the platform, distributing the sheets along the rows of chairs.

'Someone's in trouble!' a voice giggled. Her daughter, in jeans and tee shirt, slipped into the seat beside Eva. Fresh faced, slim and attractive, her eyes were the same colour as her father's, bright with mischief.

'I didn't think you were coming.'

Hope grimaced. 'I wasn't till ten minutes ago. I had to swear to Dad that I'd do my homework when I got back. I couldn't miss this though.'

Every chair was taken and people were standing, resting on walls or sitting on the floor. Eva hadn't seen such a turn out for a community event for years.

At exactly 5.30, Isaac called the meeting to order and then handed the microphone to Nick. There was a general shuffling as people settled and an air of expectation descended. Walking to the front of the stage Nick paused till there was silence. When he spoke, he had the undivided attention of the entire room.

'Thank you, everyone, for coming. I think most of you know me but, if not, my name's Nick Grigori. My brother-in-law Isaac and I head up the *20/20 Vision* Project team which, if you've not had chance to read the information sheet that young Jude over there's been distributing, has its headquarters at my department in the University, a network that extends across the world and a local office here in the village.'

'Tonight we're going to update you, our friends and neighbours, on progress with the Project and to share how other communities we link with that have similar beliefs to ours are responding to the resource challenges we all now experience. Then we want to ask for your support to address some of the undoubted difficulties we are facing in finding resources to meet basic needs because these can only be expected to worsen over time.'

'First of all I want to acknowledge the help we have received from colleagues who I have the honour to work with, in particular my Head of Department, Professor Max Greening. Without his encouragement and tireless efforts behind the scenes to clear a channel through the deluge of red tape we have to grapple with I feel sure our little ship would have run aground and capsized long ago. I give you the person who has made all this possible: Max Greening.'

A man in his late sixties in the second row got to his feet and briefly acknowledged the enthusiastic applause from an appreciative audience. He returned to his seat and, once the room was still, Nick began again.

'Thank you. Later I'm going to ask members of the University team sitting in the audience to come forward. You can collar any of us if you've got questions we don't manage to get to or you're too shy to ask in front of such a crowd.'

Nick paused, gathering his thoughts before continuing.

'As I'm sure you're all aware, having 20/20 vision means we can see as we are meant to see, as any healthy human being should. As most of you know, 2020 was also the year when the infamous Paris Climate Agreement came into being. It was meant to deal with the managing and mitigation of greenhouse gas emissions. With the benefit of hindsight we now know that, though well intentioned, that Agreement failed to deliver on its promises. We face the consequences of those failures today.

Nick nodded to Isaac who tapped the laptop. A patchwork of pictures, symbols, photographs and scenes appeared on the wall behind him. As Nick spoke, Isaac clicked on them randomly and they changed to match the descriptions he was giving. The pictures were from a range of different media sources and showed powerful and disturbing examples of human suffering. The pixilated sight of a small child lying dead on a beach was followed by one of him being held by a man in uniform, a policeman. The boy's tiny legs dressed in waterlogged blue shorts and black laced trainers hung over the man's arms. Several people in the room had to look away.

'You are seeing images from the archive that the *20/20 Project* team has been creating. It's a Time Capsule of evidence that we have been collecting from many sources for some years. It shows our growing and collective incapacity to meet worldwide humanitarian needs; the impact of war, famine and climate change. There are films, news reels, extracts from social media, books, paintings, websites still circulating but disappearing fast from the web as governments become, we believe, increasingly paranoid about being blamed for the story these tell of collective irresponsibility and failure in world leadership. We are cataloguing this evidence and creating a Programme, designed to be accessible to all.'

Nick looked across at Isaac who was staring motionless at the laptop. He paused and his brother-in-law rested clenched hands on the table. When he continued, Nick's voice was heavy with intent.

'The information that we have selected has been in the public domain for many years. Internet sites covering these events however are now being 'lost'. Governments are preparing for the political impact of what they contain. We know questions are being asked about decisions taken, or not taken, in the recent past. The 20/20 Team's vision is to contribute to the galvanising of what we believe to be a belated support for a key priority: a global response to an impending disaster.'

'We have become accustomed to unfairness and inequality over many years. In recent times in the UK, as you will be only too well aware, we have had to begin to ration certain basic requirements like food and water that in the past were considered entitlements. But in some parts of the world, as what you have just watched demonstrates, it is too late for rationing.'

Eva held her breath and realised she could have heard a pin drop. Nick paused, and, after a moment, stepped towards the audience and spoke with quiet conviction and authority.

'We are caught up in what is fast becoming a global nightmare. But this community is, in some ways, more fortunate than others. We know each other well. We have a rich heritage, a history of supporting each other and pulling together at times of shortage or oppression. You only have to look at these walls for us to be reminded of that.'

All eyes turned to the unfurled banners of workers' unions that hung around them, reminders of previous local campaigns. Colours in the fabrics were faded in places but still rich in reds and blues and golds. They could pick out images of working men and slogans that resonated across time: They did not starve; Come, let us reason together; Unity is Strength.

'I work on the *20/20 Vision* Project because I trust that the world can learn from its mistakes and tackle greed and selfishness head on. The Programme we have produced is a tool intended to help to change behaviour in the long term.'

'But we can't afford to wait for that to happen. We also have to look to our local resources, what we can do as a community, together.'

'Many of you, my wife included, have been working on community initiatives voluntarily for some time. Now we need to up our game. We know what our needs are. It is only right that we should not just talk but also take responsibility, all of us, to do something to make a difference.'

'We each have ideas for changes we can make, things we can do to tackle the challenges ahead. I know that there will be those amongst us that feel afraid. This is not going to be easy. Of course there will be times when we will struggle to know how we can best balance the universal needs that most of us share with the greater needs of the most vulnerable. But I believe that if we work together, pool our energies and resources then our community can be a beacon of hope, a shining example to others. Where we lead, others will follow.'

The applause rolled wave after wave across the room as the audience rose to its feet, carried along by the optimism in Nick's words. He looked relieved at the response, beaming a wide smile at Eva as he caught her eye. Isaac sat at the laptop watching the reactions around him and everyone started to talk at once. Hope turned to her mother, eyes shining.

'Me and my friends are going to plant apple trees right along the edge of the school field. We're starting tomorrow. Can't wait!'

The street where Nick, Eva and Hope lived had met the night before and agreed which fruit and vegetables each garden would stock. There'd been some dissenters, individuals with established allotments and small holdings who were already almost self sufficient and had no desire to change. But one of their neighbours, Terry, was a keen gardener and he'd planned out a whole year's worth of planting that, with good harvests should create produce not just for him, but enough to share with others. His enthusiasm had been contagious and although by no means everyone in the village was prepared to sacrifice the whole of their garden to the common cause, the majority were happy to contribute in some way to a plan that was slowly starting to evolve.

'We'll have gluts of food at times and that's when we can do some trading,' Terry had explained. 'Maybe swap your carrots for someone else's greens. Some of us are a bit less active than others, but there's plenty of younger folk about that'll do some digging and weeding in return for fruit and veg.'

'Don't know why we ever bothered with money,' laughed Meg an elderly resident who would need to take advantage of this option. She lived alone and had one of the biggest gardens in the street. It had been her late husband's pride and joy, full of flowers, but unlike some she'd offered it up for allotment space straight away.

Max came across to speak to Nick.

'You did well,' he grinned. Is this what you expected?'

'Yes and no, you can never be too certain how these things will work out. But we're no different from other places. Communities seem to hit a tipping point when they realise they can't go it alone and even the most hardened dissenters finally wake up to the fact that pulling together is the safest way forward.'

'Timing eh?' Max smiled. 'There's always going to be exceptions, but it would be good if everyone could get involved. The village would become even more self sufficient.'

Nick winked. 'The whole's always greater than the sum of the parts, eh?'

It would be like the old days when communities had come together to beat a common enemy, he thought. Only this time they would succeed.

Groups were gathering and exchanging ideas. The *20/20 Vision* team spent the next hour or so taking names and details of who would do what to help. Two women collected information about different care needs. It was going to be important that those with younger children or elderly dependents could also take a turn gardening, caring for livestock, helping with food distribution. Long lists were drawn up of tools, and spaces that could be shared were identified. Everyone was talking, writing, one or two were even listening. It looked chaotic to Eva.

'Great isn't it?' Nick appeared beaming at her side. 'There's so much energy.'

Eva knew from other initiatives she'd seen spring up over the years at her school that it was early days, but she didn't want to dampen his enthusiasm and knew enough to realise that without it they would never have got this far.

'How can I help? You know I'm no gardener, but I can get this lot organised if you want.'

He squeezed her arm. 'We could do with that. Isaac's a stickler for details but,' and he bent closer so only she would hear, 'between you and me your brother's got a tendency to put people off a bit.' He gave a cheeky wink and Eva couldn't help but giggle. 'We need someone that people'll find easier to work with.'

He steered her over to the table where two women were trying to collect names coming from all directions. It was obvious they were overwhelmed.

'Beth, Rachel, this is my partner, Eva. She used to be a PA before she worked at the school. Is it OK if she gives you a hand?'

Eva was there till the last stragglers had said their goodbyes. Her quiet efficiency had quickly engaged not just Beth and Rachel but two of Hope's young friends as well. By the time Nick turned out the lights and they were walking home she had established a working team, agreed times for when they would get together to run through all the information they had been given. A plan for a Community Food Programme was starting to formulate.

They would often talk of that evening in years to come. Of the evident sense of optimism that was in the room, the community's self belief and confidence in its collective strength to care for everyone.

'Someone said Community Food Programme's a bit of a mouthful,' Nick joked as he and Eva snuggled up to each other in bed that night. 'What do you think we should call the food growing work?'

Eva wrapped an arm around him and smiled sleepily, remembering an initiative from her childhood.

'How about *Incredible Edibles*?'

July 5th 2051

Nick backed into the gate, bouncing a wheelbarrow through and onto the rutted pathway. It was a cumbersome load: a shovel balanced on a heavy pile of well mulched soil. But he manoeuvred it with skill through a 180 degree turn. Setting it down he pushed up the sleeves on his faded denim shirt that hung open revealing a grubby vest. It was just possible to make out some words: *Coldplay Reunion Tour 2040*. With a grunt he flexed his arms.

After a hundred metres or so he had reached the far end of the garden, picking his way over pebbles and around puddles, his boots heavy with mud. Sunshine fell on his face, dirt had settled into the contours deepening its tan and lighting up what looked like several days of greying stubble and the easy creases of laughter lines around his eyes. A cap perched on the back of his head and a silver earring, in the shape of a dolphin, punctured his left earlobe. He whistled.

The garden stretched a good way off into the distance to a boundary fence hung about with lemon and gold honeysuckle, its heady perfume suffusing the air made damp by recent showers. A hotchpotch of overgrown bushes, piles of discarded bricks, wood torn from a dismantled shed, cans, old pots and pans, broken tools and bits of drainpipe that might one day 'come in handy' lay in front, tracing out a border. Nick paused for a moment, mopped his forehead with his cap and surveyed the scene with some pride. With the support of a growing band of volunteers this garden had been developing for over a year now. In many ways it reminded him of the allotments of his childhood. It was one of the best outcomes of the meeting they'd had that night in the Heritage Centre.

Max would have loved this. It was a tragedy his heart attack had taken him from them just at the point when everything they'd worked so hard for was coming together. Nick missed his counsel. It hadn't been straightforward to turn the initial enthusiasms of the community into organised delivery of a reliable food supply. People were never short of new ideas and it had sometimes felt necessary to let some of these run their course, even when it seemed clear to him that they were pipedreams. He knew Isaac often wanted to be more hardnosed and would grumble at energy given by individuals to what he perceived to be lost causes rather than sticking to tried and tested methods of cultivation. But Nick never tired of watching his neighbours, friends and family working together and having a go at something that might just make a difference or create a new food supply that would add some variety to their lives.

'If you don't try, you don't learn,' he would often say in response to his brother-in-law's criticisms.

People of all ages were in the garden digging, fetching, picking, tasting. Children were becoming dirtier by the minute. It was a hive of purposeful activity. As he watched, a little boy and girl, he guessed just out of nappies, carried a box of newly picked strawberries to a table. Their mother walked alongside them, clapping her hands in encouragement. When they reached the table a couple of women took the box and each popped a ripe berry into the children's wide open mouths, turned upwards in expectation like the beaks of baby birds. They bit down hard, white teeth contrasting with the redness of the fruit, reaching up with muddy fingers to wipe their chins as the juices overflowed and dribbled past their darting tongues.

Compared with other parts of the country and some of the communities with which they were still in contact who were trying to be similarly self sufficient, in this first year they had been very lucky. Signs of a good harvest were everywhere, the garden bursting with a lush cornucopia of produce dripping from every stem and bough. Mother Earth's womb had swollen and she had delivered in a riot of colour an abundance that was beyond their wildest expectations. The pinks and blues and purples and whites of spring had given way to reds and greens, oranges and yellows. They would still need to be careful, but should at least fare well this winter.

Nick joined a group working on clearing a large patch of weeds and rubble in a shaded corner tucked away from the main thoroughfare. Behind the panting and heaving, a clear sense of purposeful planning was evident. They were a band of brothers. In a matter of hours a space had been cleared, outlines pegged out and building materials gathered. By the end of the afternoon a rudimentary henhouse had begun to appear, recreated from the flotsam and jetsam scattered about.

It was a warm afternoon, the air beginning to shimmer in the heat and Nick was parched. It occurred to him that it was perfect for sharing a beer on the beach, and that in his youth that's probably what he'd have been doing. Interesting how priorities changed, he mused.

Ellie arrived with welcome jugs of pressed apple juice. Throwing their various tools onto the turned rich, dark soil individuals either perched or leaned on anything available, and gulped it down.

'Still doing what makes you happy?' she asked, taking in the sweat making her brother's vest stick to his skin and the long smear of mud down his face where he'd tried to wipe it from his brow.

Nick grinned at his sister and laughed. 'What do you think?'

She smiled back, took the empty cup and wrapping her other arm round his waist surveyed their handiwork.

'It's looking good. You've got loads done.'

Nick nodded, aware of the heat trickling down his shoulders. He wasn't a great gardener, he hadn't a clue how to build a hen house, but he could always lend his energy to a project and lead from the front.

'Teamwork,' he grinned.

Later that evening, as the sun was setting and the air chilled people collected around a bonfire. The stack of branches, bushes and leaves had grown over the weeks and now stood like a wigwam, crackling and pulsing, throwing heat and light across the faces of those gathering in tangled knots on the ground.

Nick stretched out on an old rug, Eva's head in his lap. He could see Hope to his right. She was with a group of friends chatting, drawing her long hair round her shoulders and back to the front across to one side. It was an unconscious movement that reminded him so much of Eva when he had first met her. He felt the familiar tension he was sure most fathers of beautiful young women would understand: a sense of both pride and protectiveness.

One of the boys had a ukulele and was starting to pick out a folk tune which the others began to sing, tripping over the notes but every now and then hitting some harmonies that added a resonance to the words. Out of the lengthening shadows came the sound of a penny whistle and then one of the women produced a fiddle and brought other strains to the music lilting through the trees. Multi coloured ribbons, bits of bunting and jangles of pebbles and carved wood twirled and twinkled, chiming from branches dappled by the late sunlight, the air heavy with the perfume of ripe vegetation. Ellie was handing round warm bread and roasted vegetables were starting to appear from the embers, pungent with smoke. Nick leant forward and kissed the top of Eva's head. There were always going to be challenges and he was under no illusions, they could never relax fully, but just for now it was becoming a magical evening and he wanted to enjoy it.

He noticed Jude sitting alone on the opposite side of the circle from Hope. Ellie wandered across and squatting down offered her son something from her tray of food but he shook his head without looking up. She stayed by his side for a few minutes until one of the other women indicated that there was more ready to pass around and she went back to the cooking area, leaving Jude to himself again. Nick looked round for Isaac.

'Where's your brother? He's not still working on the Programme is he?'

Eva nodded. 'I looked in on him before I came down. He's the only one still there. I told him to leave it for now but you know what he's like. He just wants to get it finished.'

Nick groaned. 'I'd better go and get him. He'll be there all night otherwise.'

He lifted Eva's shoulders and lowered her onto the rug where she stretched out and then curled like a sleepy child.

'Won't be long, save me a beer.'

******   ******   ******

As he opened the gate he could see Isaac in the distance making his way home. Nick broke into a jog and as he got closer called to him. On the second attempt Isaac heard, stopped and waited for his brother-in-law to catch up.

'Everyone's in the garden. Are you coming down for something to eat with us?'

Nick noted the way Isaac stooped. There were puffy bags under his eyes and lines appeared more etched into his skin. He felt guilty for leaving the responsibility of archiving for the Programme with him. The light was fading and Nick couldn't be sure if Isaac was registering his concern or, in his tiredness, brushing it away.

'It's fine, I'll get something at home.'

'How's it going?'

'Better than I'd expected to be honest' Nick sighed with relief. He wasn't in the mood to deal with martyrdom.

'Managed to get hold of a few of the people in London and Washington and they've released some of the more sensitive early policy statements and climate footage to us before it gets taken down for good. That's all uploaded and protected now and ready to go.'

'Great, mate. Well done.'

Isaac glanced round and came close to Nick's ear to speak. 'Think it's helping that some of the bigger players have woken up to the reality of the situation. It's as if they're falling over themselves to do something by way of an apology now. It's too bloody late of course. They know we're screwed.'

Nick nodded. He'd worked late himself the night before on the Programme and with one of the medical team reviewed some of the international health studies that were now starting to circulate more openly. Fertility rates were falling steadily across the world and though there were plenty of theories being offered for these trends no one seemed to be able to explain why they were happening. Until recently the exact figures had been top secret but some studies were showing this drop in birth rate was becoming more and more widespread. Questions were also being asked about the steady rise in auto immune conditions like Type 1 diabetes, multiple sclerosis and rheumatoid arthritis and proposing potential links with chemicals that had become hidden deep within the food chain.

'Once the dominoes really start to fall, we always suspected cracks would open up in the walls this information's been sealed behind and come flooding out.'

'No government's going to want to break their cover first and own responsibility for covering up knowledge like this. The implications are potentially so big,' Isaac responded angrily. 'They probably haven't been properly acted upon for years. And smaller states tied into agreements with bigger players won't have had as much power, but they'll know they still could be blamed for what's been happening.'

Nick sighed. 'You know what some people say: *The saddest words of all: If only, but too late.*'

Isaac had played cat and mouse for months, working through layers of skulduggery to reach undercover sources and open doors to information on corporate betrayals and greed swept under mats for years. The evidence of a long standing denial of an impending doom stretching back well into the mid twentieth century was everywhere.

In searching for something to say Nick found himself tumbling out an excited description of his day's work. Isaac was silent.

'You don't seem too impressed?'

They had settled on a bench in need of a long overdue repaint. Shadows were lengthening and Nick could hear the wind rustling the leaves in the branches that hung above them. A solitary gull swooped and dipped on the last warm currents before nightfall, disappearing into the distance.

Isaac muttered through clenched teeth. 'It just all seems so pointless.'

Nick was in no mood for another of Isaac's diatribes. They'd worked hard in the garden all day doing something positive, together. He was worn out. Couldn't Isaac at least be happy for that? A henhouse and harvest might not change the big picture, but it was something. They'd made certain of food for the winter. And what about Jude? Surely he had a responsibility to show positivity, spend some time with his son? He couldn't leave that all up to Ellie.

He stood. 'Well, I'm going down to eat with the rest. Are you coming or not?'

Isaac slumped where he sat. After a pause he looked up and stared ahead, outstretched arms resting across the back of the chair. Nick took out a tin and rolled a cigarette, holding it out to Isaac who shook his head.

'Wish I could be more like you.'

Nick struck a match and inhaled slowly. He lowered himself back onto the bench.

'How do you mean?'

Isaac seemed to be turning words over in his head.

'You're calm, you sleep at night. You don't seem to get angry at the mess out there.'

Nick tipped back his head and gave a half smile.

'What's the point? I'm trying not to look too far ahead, just count my blessings. We need to keep positive for the kids.'

He could hear Isaac's breathing, deep and heavy.

'It's the kids I worry about. Feels like we're duping them into believing everything's going to be OK, when we know it's not.'

Nick twisted round and stared at his brother-in-law. He didn't want to hear this.

'We don't 'know' that Isaac. None of us 'know' anything.'

Isaac continued to look ahead and then turned and gripped Nick's arms so hard that his nails dug into his skin and made him wince.

'I think we do.'

Three Years Later

September 30th 2054

What a difference a few years could make. Changes that took place within the community as each month passed were steady but on the surface caused only small ripples. Some families moved away, a few people died. The decline in numbers was slow and at first they were able to adapt to the impact. When they looked back probably there was inevitability to the direction they were travelling that they might have seen sooner, but they had perhaps not wanted to believe the evidence.

'Why can't we just get ahead?' Nick said to Eva one day.

They had all tried their hardest, but each time something had seemed to go wrong. It rained when it needed to be sunny, and when it was hot it was unbearable. Their earlier optimism had evaporated like mist.

At first they'd sown seeds, harvested fruit and vegetables, thrived. Nick had been able to rally the troops, build confidence and plan. They used three simple techniques-education and example and effort. It should have been possible to grow the numbers in the village, to bring in new people with a similar set of values and attitudes to their own. Things wouldn't always be difficult, there was always hope. All they needed was a bit of luck.

Nick was focused on delivery, and with no time to scan the horizon, had missed what was happening right in front of him.

'Have you noticed how few butterflies there are this year?' Eva mentioned it in passing and he started to pay attention. She was right. He hadn't seen a single one, or bees for that matter. The mornings were eerily quiet these days whereas it was not so long ago that he remembered bird song waking him at dawn.

The community itself was changing, and it wasn't because of the weather. Something more serious was wrong. Not just with the replenishment of the food stocks and wildlife, but themselves. He stood at the window one morning and watched people setting out for their day's activities and tried to work it out.

'Where are the babies?' he muttered under his breath and counted half a dozen couples who could reasonably have been expected to have started a family by now. When he asked Eva about it she bit her lip.

'What's up? Is there something you're not telling me?'

She lay the book she'd been reading face down on the table and reaching out took hold of his hand.

'I didn't want to say anything; I knew you'd just worry.'

'What about?'

Wrapping his hand in both of hers she pulled him close.

'You've worked so hard, we all have.'

'What's going on Eva?'

She stared out of the window. A young woman was making her way across the road towards the garden. She seemed preoccupied, not responding to the greetings of others that passed her.

'I wish I knew.'

Eva's eyes followed the woman until she disappeared round the corner and then she turned to Nick, her face grave.

'You see Carolyn there? I'm not supposed to tell anyone, but two weeks ago she had a miscarriage.'

Nick was shocked. He'd not realised she was pregnant, but he had wondered whether Carolyn and Mike would have kids. They'd been together more than three years and he'd often thought when he'd seen them with someone else's children what great parents they'd make.

'I'm so sorry to hear that. How far along was she?'

'Eight weeks.'

'Just eight weeks?'

He didn't want to sound crass.

'And before you say anything, it doesn't matter how early it was, she was still pregnant.'

'I know, I wasn't meaning...'

Eva gripped the window ledge behind her. He noticed with a shock how white her knuckles were.

'The last three times she'd made it to twelve.'

She registered the look of horror, let go of the ledge and folded her arms tight across her chest.

'Three times? You mean...?'

'Yes, this was their fourth pregnancy and she's miscarried them all.'

They decided to get some air. The tide was out and they could walk along the shore on the hard damp sand across uncovered rocks slimy with weed and normally hidden from view. Little pools of sea water sheltered tiny crabs scuttling out their lives making their invisible homes under rocks and in shells amongst the dark rubbery fronds wafting in the currents. They clambered out on the rocks as far as they could and sat watching white horses cresting as the waves rolled and tumbled towards them.

'Why didn't you tell me before?'

Eva kept her eyes focused on the horizon.

'She asked me not to. I think they feel the fewer people that know the less real it seems.'

Eva had always wanted more children, so had Ellie, but for some reason it just hadn't happened. Hope had been enough for him, but he didn't deny he wouldn't have minded a son as well. It just wasn't to be.

'The thing is Nick, Carolyn and Mike aren't the only ones to have lost babies.'

'Who else has?'

There was a long pause before she responded. As she reeled off the names it became apparent that an invisible Angel of Death that they'd known for some years was at work elsewhere also hovered over their own village.

'Reports were circulating some time ago about falling fertility,' said Nick. 'There'd been questions asked in certain quarters for years. We managed to get hold of some of the papers for the Project. Lots of speculation about possible causes but nothing anyone could prove, let alone do anything to stop. They don't know if it was some sort of pollution or something to do with lifestyle.'

He groaned. 'We need more research.'

Eva had long been the confidant of so many of their friends in the community, trusted for her ability to keep secrets. She had been containing this knowledge for months. Eva looked at Nick, her normally bright eyes tired and moist with tears.

'It's so unfair.'

That evening, when Hope had gone to bed, they talked again.

'Isaac's worried about our food stores,' said Nick. 'With so little coming through in deliveries from elsewhere we've been becoming more and more reliant on what we've grown ourselves and managed to squirrel away.'

'I know. I looked in on one of the stores yesterday. It was almost empty.'

'Did you see the family that drove through this morning on their way north? The kids looked like they were starving. I gave them some bread and that bag of apples in the larder.'

Eva bit her lip. Nick knew what she was thinking. That was their last bag.

Nick could see what was happening, but changes in attitudes were coming with great speed and he felt powerless to stop them. The energies of the village were increasingly being directed into protecting the food they had from others less fortunate or, as he'd heard them described, *less deserving, more irresponsible,* people who had nothing. He suspected more and more families would become nomadic, refugees, drought and famine in the south moving them northwards, begging for food and shelter where they could find them.

They had elected a committee from the community to oversee the work that they did together. Meetings had often become fractious as pressures built. Nick had felt the tension in priorities between himself and Isaac. Once undercurrents, these differences began to play out in public.

'We can't force people to put time into supporting the community as a whole,' he'd pointed out time and again at meetings. 'We've got to win them round, build their motivation.'

'That's all very well, Nick,' Isaac had snapped back. 'But some of us don't see it like that. We haven't got enough for those of us that do volunteer, who work to support this community on top of our normal work. What makes you think people are going to be willing to feed people that don't pull their weight?'

As tensions grew, keeping enough produce safe to feed the village had started to become a priority. The work of Incredible Edibles was renamed Community Food Security. At some point, Nick couldn't put his finger on quite when, they had dropped the word 'Community'. Strangers and visitors who had previously been offered help were regarded with increasing suspicion that at times overflowed into open resentment.

'We've got to patrol the stores and safeguard their contents from starving scavengers,' Isaac explained at one of the committee meetings. 'This is our food, not theirs.'

Fortified with barbed wire, the stores contained food, becoming impregnable larders whose doors were padlocked and chained, their contents protected for the consumption only of those who had volunteered any spare time that they had to produce what was inside.

They were secure vaults. Food Banks.

******   ******   ******

One night Nick was on guard with Jude. All the men took a turn to watch, working in pairs to patrol the village boundaries, catching up on sleep during the day. The schedule meant there were fewer of them available for heavy manual work and they were falling behind with essential repairs and replanting. Nick and the other men had discussed this. They knew that the community would soon reach a tipping point. If they hadn't known before what the future would hold, they were starting to now.

It was chilly and damp. A stiff breeze rustled the trees and bushes, clouds scudded across a dark sky. The moon was hidden and the sense of the earth closing down, lying in bedraggled rags and tatters, beginning its process of deep hibernation, hung in the air like the atmosphere of a forlorn fairground at the end of the summer season. Memories were buried away, tumbled into hidden alcoves and recesses in the mind's eye, ready to reappear as stories told before campfires accompanied by dark winter nights.

The regular scouting party had returned at nightfall from sweeping the area with nothing to report, so they hoped this would be a routine watch. Nick and Jude had done a first tour of inspection, checking fences and wires, resetting traps, rattling doors and testing the heavy bolts and padlocks fixed like clenched fists at every entry point. Now they were huddled under a sheet of old tarpaulin, listening to the sound of rain dripping above them, peering into the darkness and straining to hear.

Jude had grown into a watchful young man, speaking when spoken to, but articulate and wary. There was something about the way he held himself back in company that troubled Nick. He sensed in his nephew something other than shyness, more an unease, a fear of making a mistake, of criticism. Yet he was reliable and dedicated to the work of the village, never missing a shift or slacking in his duties.

'You must be proud of Jude,' he'd once said to Isaac as they worked late pulling together the final archive material for the Programme. As usual he got a less than enthusiastic response with Isaac grumbling and rehearsing Jude's various oversights and omissions. Nick looked at his nephew out of the corner of his eye, sharpening the long knife resting on his lap. He was a good kid, diligent and dutiful. He didn't have Hope's flair and creativity, but he was loyal, a reliable pair of hands to have beside you if you were ever in a fight.

'Time for another patrol?'

Jude nodded and stood, pausing to slip the knife into the scabbard hanging at his waist. As he did so, they both froze. Through the wind and creaking of branches they had heard a heavy thud and then a low grunt.

Jude slid the knife from its sheath, holding it upright in front of him. Both men knelt, ready to spring, then began to inch themselves forward.

The movement had come from the area where a large pit covered with branches and leaves had been camouflaged to make it look like the solid garden floor.

They peered over the edge. Something was crumpled and moaning in the darkness and whatever it was had been hurt.

'Get a torch,' Nick whispered and Jude slipped away, returning with a large black object. They edged towards the lip of the pit and Nick flicked on the switch.

Everything happened at once. He felt a rush from behind as too late Jude shouted out a warning. Nick plummeted over the side and tumbling through the air, he landed on top of the shapeless form below him, which collapsed and went still. For a moment he was winded, but he became aware of the sound of a fierce struggle above. Jude was being attacked. He had to get out and help.

Nick searched the pit's walls for some sort of hand or foothold. He could hear blows being rained down, punches thrown, yelps of pain, but had no way of knowing what was happening.

As he stood in the centre of the circle staring upwards there was a sudden yowl of agony from above and a body spread-eagled its way over the edge and cart wheeled down towards him. He pressed himself hard against the wall just in time.

'Nick! Are you OK?'

It was Jude's voice.

'Yeah, I'm fine. Can you get a rope?'

The clouds parted and the moon lit up the scene for an instant. There were two bodies at his feet; one with a neck twisted backwards, the other with a knife sunk up to its shaft handle deep in its chest.

October 1st 2054

News of the ambush spread like wildfire through the village overnight. By mid morning everyone knew something of what had happened, but rumour was rife and a vicelike fear choked the community into silence. Nick called to check on Jude in the morning, passing no one in the streets. This was a time to keep your loved ones in clear view. He took Isaac to one side.

'We've got to take hold of things and get people together before we have mass hysteria on our hands.'

'Fine-I'll get the word out. One o'clock?'

It was a Council of War. They convened, as usual, in the old Heritage Centre, the scene over the years of so many debates and decisions. Remnants of past celebrations and anniversaries clung in tatters to walls, fading memories of a distant optimism. Once brightly coloured flags and banners now hung with signs of damp and musty decay speckling their surfaces. The whole place had an air of sadness and neglect. Nick had known for some time the image was not good for morale, but with other priorities had lacked the energy to do anything about it.

Isaac offered to address the audience and Nick, exhausted, was only too happy to let him take the lead. Through the throbbing drumbeat of a headache caused by having had no sleep he could not concentrate on the words, but he got the sense of the message: fear, vulnerability, insufficient resources. These were the themes and Isaac was driving them home.

'Last night was a warning. It may have been an isolated attack, but who knows how long it will be before we have more? We cannot hope to continue as we are forever. This village, our community, is no longer safe here. We are already diverting much of our limited manpower into protecting what little we have. Strangers want to steal what is rightfully ours, food we have sweated and toiled to grow. Of course, they have needs. But we have our own mouths to feed, our own precious children and families to care for. Our enemies are becoming desperate and will stop at nothing.'

There were uneasy murmurs of assent. Nick cast his eyes over the room. Were these really the people he had grown up with, friends and neighbours he had thought of almost as family? Once upon a time their mismatched outfits, haphazard approach to health and safety had given them an air of artistry and creative individuality. It hadn't taken long for them to lose that optimism, now they looked more like third world street beggars. They wore a look of permanent greyness, their skin, hair and nails all lacking the lustre of regular rejuvenation, eyes dull and dead. Poverty did this to people. He caught sight of his reflection in one of the windows and realised with a shock how much his own appearance had changed. Dirty and dishevelled, he looked old.

Jude was sitting next to his father. His face was scratched and bruised, one eye angry and blackened. He was impassive, following Isaac's every word, only darting momentary glances out to the audience and shifting in his seat when his father drew attention to his part in the previous night's events. Isaac placed a hand on Jude's shoulder and he flinched. Nick, not for the first time, felt sorry for his nephew.

The room was stuffy, the air heavy with the smell of sweat. Nick couldn't breathe.

Just as he thought he might faint, Hope's voice rang out from the back of the room.

'You're wrong.'

Nick made to stand, but felt Eva's restraining hand. All eyes in the room had turned to his daughter.

Isaac looked Hope up and down in silence. There was something in his manner that made Nick clench his fists. Hope didn't flinch.

'Wrong?'

She turned to the crowd, took a deep breath and spoke with calm assurance. Before Nick's eyes, his daughter came of age.

'If we were starving wouldn't we fight for our families as these people that came last night were ready to fight for theirs? Why should we think that our rights matter more, that we are more entitled? There has to be a better way for us to live than in fear: running and hiding.'

Isaac's response was instant.

'Your generosity does you credit, Hope,' he sneered. 'But,' turning to the rest of the room 'the facts can speak for themselves.

Our community is shrinking, we are all getting older. Protecting resources for ourselves is not selfish, it is pragmatic.'

They talked all through the afternoon and well into the evening. Even without the attack, they had to acknowledge that the village was at a crossroads. If it was to survive they needed a place that was easier to defend.

As night fell they came to a decision. They would have to move.

Having discussed several suggestions one place emerged as the best option. It was the best part of a day's journey further north, an island cut off for long periods of the day and night by an incoming tide and only accessible by a causeway from the mainland. Nick and Ellie knew it well: they had visited often as children. Some of the villagers had friends and family living there and for some time they had been considering joining them. The attack was just the catalyst they needed.

The island was an ancient place with a rich history. Although it had long since become more secular, in the past, it had been known as a spot where people of faith had established a community, seeking to live a life based on beliefs they held dear, shielded from the rest of the world. That history resonated with their own situation in a way that they had never expected.

Nick got to his feet.

'There are already families and relatives of some of us living on this island. If we are to be welcomed, to join with them then we must never forget that these are people who have the same needs as us. For it's their home, not ours. To be accepted we must give thought to how we can present ourselves as an asset, not a threat. What we can share: materials, knowledge, our skills and experiences.'

The irony of the situation escaped no one. At a stroke, in any new environment they would be transformed from residents with homes they could call their own, to refugees.

Eva glanced around the room. These people were part of her history, a story that stretched back several generations in some of their memories. She looked across to her in laws remembering how Sarai had adored Hope from the moment she first set eyes on her. She had helped to fill the void left by the loss of her own daughter Mia, one of the first victims of the growing and mysterious fragility in health that was now so much a part of all of their lives. Sarai had been a force to be reckoned with, fighting and battling every inch of the way to prise any drop of help she could to try to save Mia. But it had been to no avail. Now Sarai was one of their elders, someone Eva turned to for comfort and wisdom, a steady rock to feel anchored to in a stormy sea.

With no context, no history, no story to reflect on, how would the island community view her mother-in-law? There was no getting away from it. She was old. Would she be perceived as an asset or a liability? Isaac often referred to members of the community who were vulnerable as 'passengers'.

When would it be her turn to be judged and found wanting?

October 5th 2054

'Jude, bury the two attackers,' Isaac ordered. 'Leave them in the pit and cover them there. There's no need to mark the grave.'

With a quick nod, Jude slipped from the room. Watching him leave Hope felt for her cousin. It would be a grisly task. She was relieved when two other men got to their feet and followed him out.

Jack Errington, one of the committee members, stood up. 'I'll ride to the island and speak to those in charge to find out how they'd view new arrivals. My sister, Naomi, is one of the island's leaders.' Before anyone could stop him he left. When he returned the news, to all of their immense relief, was positive.

The village took just three days to pack. They had no way of knowing if the intruders would be searched for when they did not return or if any that might follow would be more prepared and better armed. They could not take that risk.

Isaac with Jude took control of the *20/20* archive making sure that as much of the story as possible was uploaded into a memory stick. The laptop was wrapped and packed.

'We need to leave something behind,' said Hope. She selected a small brick structure on the cliff top that had been used to store unwanted tools. It stood on a hillock tucked out of the wind. It was filled with artefacts and images, stories and objects that were so much part of their lives, wanting it to be visible to anyone that passed by, but secure and watertight. Hope selected seeds and attached descriptions of all that they had learned about the soil, the weather, the surrounding area in case this would be knowledge that could help others that might want to try where they had failed.

When it was finished, Hope carved a single word into a simple wooden plaque and nailed it to the front: *Community*.

The women and children selected and packed the most precious of their possessions, all the time with an eye not just on whether they meant something to them, but also how they might be perceived to those that they hoped would take them in. Some of these decisions about what to take were hard, saying much about what they valued by way of memories: a photograph, a ring, a lost child's first shoe.

On the final night the entire village gathered for one last meal. Each horse drawn wagon and their few remaining trucks were packed for the journey. Animals had been gathered into pens ready to be herded to their new homes, everyone had picked out a presentable outfit to wear in the morning. Those that were going to join family members there already were reassuring of the welcome they would receive. All being well they should reach the island before nightfall and, if the scouts had also done their job, by the time the main party arrived, they would all be assured safe passage across the causeway.

Nick paced round the encampment and looked through the piles of produce heaped high on the wagons and in bags ready for the morning. This was impression management on a grand scale. Everyone knew it was not the time to show need or weakness.

Seeing Hope making some final preparations he walked over to her. She had worked hard, comforting and challenging in equal measure, trying to make decisions that would serve them all well. On seeing him she smiled a greeting.

'Dad, are you going to say anything to everyone before we go to bed tonight?'

Nick hugged her, wondering when she had grown to be so wise.

Within half an hour the community had gathered around a final campfire. In the flickering light Nick picked out familiar faces. He felt none of his youthful optimism, but instead a weight of responsibility for leading these people, his friends.

'Tomorrow will be a day none of us will forget. We take with us many things-memories of our struggles, of our successes and, yes, of our failures. Those are the memories we all hold in our minds and hearts.'

He held up the memory stick.

'This carries the story of our past. We guard that history in the hope that one day we will be able to use it to teach those that follow. But for now, we have prepared well for the journey. Tonight our scouts will go ahead to check the path for us. They will need to have their wits about them and be careful. Let us wish them luck.'

At this point Hope, Jude and a group of around ten young men and women stood and received the good wishes and embraces of those present. Eva and Nick had tears in their eyes as they held their daughter in their arms.

'Be careful, my darling,' whispered Eva.

Nick saw Ellie clinging to Jude while Isaac stood by. When his mother let him go Jude turned to his father, took a step towards him, but hesitated and then held out his hand. Once their goodbyes had been said and each of the scouts was armed with the knives and rifles that had been set aside for their protection, they slipped away into the darkness.

The Island
October 6th 2054

Whether it was the scouts that had done their job well or the size of their convoy, the rest of the village had no need for the weapons they had kept with them for their own security. They started out the next morning and the journey through the countryside passed without incident.

The day had dawned misty, but by mid morning the skies had cleared and they could see a good way into the distance to grey blue hilltops. As the day progressed Eva's thoughts were on Hope, impatient to know that she was safe. Nick did his best to reassure her.

'She's with the others and they know to be careful,' he said squeezing her hand in his.

'I know, but I can't help worrying. I just want to see her.'

The convoy had received its instructions.

'Keep to back roads and avoid villages,' Isaac had ordered. It was a good plan and even though they moved at the pace of the slowest vehicle they managed to reach the causeway to the island by early evening. The tide had just turned and the way across lay ahead of them cutting over an exposed sea bed.

Jude, Hope and the other scouts were waiting. Eva cried with relief and as they came to a halt she jumped out of the truck, ran to her daughter and flung her arms around her. A group of islanders stood alongside these young people and three of them stepped forward, arms outstretched. The two men and one woman were wrapped in layers of warm clothing and bore themselves with the dignity of people used to receiving respect. They appeared to be a similar age to Nick's parents. Both the men had grey hair and the woman's was silver, pinned up loosely, framing clear bright eyes while a few strands rested on her slim shoulders

'Welcome, welcome all of you,' said the taller of the men and there followed much hand shaking and hugging and warm smiles of comfort and reassurance. Nick felt stinging tears. Perhaps this would, in the end, prove to be a good choice and all would be well. He had to stop himself from falling to his knees and kissing the feet of each person hurrying along the causeway to greet them. Instead of being wary or fearful of strangers as they had, in spite of the reassurances they had been given, half expected, these people were bringing blankets, small trailers, the help of extra pairs of hands a welcome way to ease the tiredness of the new arrivals. He marvelled at the hospitality and yearned to understand it. But for now, he just felt gratitude and relief.

The path was marked with stakes that would have guided travellers for centuries. The distance could be measured in hundreds of yards, but this was a journey they knew had been made by men and women for thousands of years. Glad of the chance to breathe the sea air, Nick handed the wheel of his vehicle to one of the other men and made the crossing by foot.

They were led to the centre of the village where they gathered in front of a collection of grey stone cottages, their slate black roofs shining in the gathering evening sunset. An ancient Celtic cross bore testimony to the island's heritage.

'My name is Naomi,' said the woman who had first greeted them in warm, clear tones. 'I'm Jack's sister. This island has long been a refuge for those seeking shelter. We decided long ago that here we would do everything in our power to maintain that tradition. In recent years we have been able to provide safe harbouring for many who have passed this way. Some have stayed; some have chosen to move on. That is their decision, as it will be yours. For tonight we will make you as comfortable as we can and then, in the morning, when you are refreshed we can talk. But first, you must all be very tired and hungry.'

Nick watched as these strangers set about drawing them all into their community. Everything was conducted with a grace and sensitivity that touched and warmed even the hardest heart. He couldn't help but smile at the sight of Jude, normally hesitant and cautious in new company, allowing himself to be led by two small children through a doorway into a barn set about with lanterns and mattresses, bowls of fruit and warm blankets. Hope and the other scouts were helping the youngest children and the most elderly down from trucks and introducing them to families flowing forward to greet them with warm hospitality. All too quickly the square was almost empty as every available dwelling opened its doors to absorb these guests.

He and Eva were given a room belonging to a young couple who insisted on surrendering their own bed for them while they slept downstairs on a sofa. Such kindness from strangers was something they hadn't known for years. It touched them both.

'It's so precious to meet with people that can be generous,' Eva whispered as they lay in bed.

Nick murmured in agreement. They'd been like this once. Caring for people, whoever they were.

'When did it all start to change, Nick? What made us stop thinking of ourselves as all the same?'

He didn't have an answer, but safe and warm they both drifted towards unconsciousness. Sometimes it was just easier not to think.

October 7th 2054

They woke to an unmistakeable smell that Nick had almost forgotten.

Frying bacon.

They emerged into the village square, fed and nourished and filled with an unfamiliar sense of well being, to the kind of scene that they had both half expected never to witness again. This was a community that worked and played hard, sharing whatever they had, even with strangers.

'This is weird. Everyone's so busy, but they all look happy,' said Eva. 'Is it drugs?'

Nick laughed, recognising the power of undertaking purposeful, creative activity with others.

They wandered around the village, being greeted by islanders emerging to face the day and reached a large single storey building much newer than the other constructions on the island. An ornate, carved sign indicated that this was the Gathering House. As they hesitated, the door opened and Naomi emerged with her two companions from the night before, Mark and John. They greeted Eva and Nick, gently enquired about the quality of their night's sleep, seeking reassurances that they were refreshed and felt ready to talk.

Inside, the building felt dressed rather than furnished. Wild flowers and grasses had been placed on window ledges and walls covered with beautiful pieces of art work, collages and tapestries, water colours and sculptures, celebrating the beauty in the simplicity and abundance of the natural world.

Isaac joined them, and then Jude and Hope. Soon there was a gathering of around a hundred. Naomi turned to Nick.

'I'm guessing you would all like to see a bit more of the island before you make a decision about whether this is the right place for you all to settle? It's going to be a fine day so you'll be seeing it at its best.'

They divided into small groups and each set off in different directions to explore. They agreed to meet back at the centre for lunch.

Naomi led Nick, Eva, Hope, Jude, Ellie and Isaac through the village and along to an ancient church. As they walked she told them stories about every landmark, pointing to the castle that had once been a fortress and now stood like a brooding presence at one end of the island linking past and present. She wove a narrative that was informative but also reflected her long standing relationship and fondness for both the people and the place.'

'I was born here,' she explained. 'The church is built on a site that has been sacred for hundreds of years. The island has always been a place where people have come to live, to seek safety, to rest and work. I have always felt it had a special atmosphere, a sense of being connected to the ideas and beliefs of many that lived here in the past. I believe those values have influenced how we have come to choose to live now.'

Inside the church, light flooded through an exquisite stained glass window, the beams gilding the well worn wooden pews, dusty grey stonework and memorials to local people whose lives had graced the community and earned the right to have their names carved into the walls.

A heavy wooden door drew Isaac's attention and he asked Naomi about it.

'It's our crypt,' she said. 'Just a small room, windowless but unusual because it has a lock. We have very little need for keys in our community, but there can be times, of course, when it is necessary to keep something very special in a secure place.'

Isaac kept his eyes on Naomi but when she turned away he nudged Nick and winked. Nick knew what he meant. The crypt could be the ideal place for the laptop.

December 2054

Over the next few weeks they became assimilated into the island's simple rhythms. The kindness and generosity they were shown by their hosts soon began to work its magic.

'I can feel myself starting to breathe again,' Eva said to Nick one morning. He knew what she meant. The provisions they had brought were shared with their hosts. In the main they slept in spare rooms in cottages and guest houses that had for generations provided accommodation for holiday makers spending a tranquil break in what had been a peaceful retreat.

Eva continued to be reassured by the attitude shown towards the elderly. To her delight she saw not many but at least some younger children and there were sufficient numbers in the community as a whole to give a healthy balance between those that could work and those who brought other attributes that were valued: knowledge, wisdom and gravitas. Sarai and Abe found new friends and their spirits seemed to lift in the atmosphere of acceptance and respect.

'How are you doing? Is it what you expected?' she'd asked Sarai at the end of a day where everyone had been preparing for the upcoming Christmas festivities. Sarai had worked with three other older women weaving foliage, gathered from far and wide by the children, into festive table decorations for the special meal they understood that the whole island would share. Their fingers had coaxed and curled variegated ivy, holly sharp with thorns and adorned with berries and tiny sprigs of pine into fragrant nests encircling candles and cones, all the time chatting and laughing, recounting memories of Christmases long past.

Her mother-in-law took Eva's hand and squeezed it. Her skin was like dry paper, but cool and soft.

'Never better, love. Couldn't be happier.'

Everyone was busy, productive and confident. Look outs watched the sea and land for evidence of other human activity, but very little energy went into self protection or defence. There was a powerful confidence embedded deep within the culture of this community. It seemed to give them courage.

Nick asked Naomi about it one afternoon as they sat on upturned lobster pots mending nets that would soon be packed away for the winter.

'Aren't you worried that you might be attacked like we were?' he asked.

Naomi smiled. 'Ah, the art of worrying, how many hours have I wasted on that! It's simple, Nick. We made a choice some time ago, as leaders and a community that we would try not to be afraid of what we might lose, but instead be thankful for what each day brings. Whatever Fate threw at us we would try to accept. Our attitude would be 'Bring it on.'

'If we were to lie awake at night, cowed with thoughts of 'what if...' our energies, which are limited already, would be sapped even further. Fear would make us wary of strangers; divert our minds to protectionism, to clinging on tight to what little we have. You can see we don't have riches, we lead a simple life. We would never have opened our doors to your little colony if we'd given in to negative thoughts, and we'd have missed out on so much as a consequence. You've enriched us with your knowledge; brought skills and resources we could never generate ourselves. Yes, it was a risk to open our doors to strangers, but we calculated that it would be a far greater one to keep them closed.'

Was this wise? Pragmatic? Nick wasn't sure. Although he could not deny he had been afraid at times back in their village and that the constant bickering between himself and Isaac had worn him down, in spite of the feelings of impending doom they had experienced only one actual attack.

Nick wanted to return Naomi's trust with similar generosity. Christmas was coming, maybe that would give him an opportunity.

He ran his idea first past Eva.

'I want to tell Naomi about the Programme.'

'Of course, you'd be crazy not to. She'll love what you and the others have been doing. It's part of you, a legacy.'

Reassured by Eva's enthusiasm, Nick's knew that his next step was to speak to Isaac. Always more wary than Nick and less willing to trust others, he suspected he would be a tougher nut to crack. But it was not as hard a task as he'd expected.

'I was thinking that the crypt would be the logical place to house the laptop. It's out of sight, dry and quiet,' said Isaac. 'People could access the Programme and learn from it, build their awareness of what's been going on.'

Relieved by Isaac's apparent positivity, Nick pressed on.

'Exactly. These islanders could pass the information around everyone that lives here now and may do in the future.'

'Have you met Neil yet?' asked Isaac. 'Chap in his late thirties, lives with his partner and parents in the cottage on the corner down by the shore? I was chatting to him last week. Apparently he used to be in IT security when he was in London. Said himself he was a bit of a geek, but he knows his stuff. Had a lot to do with preventing hacking apparently, very knowledgeable about how to get round firewalls. He came up here to be with his parents about five years ago, brought some of his kit with him. You know, I bet he could help us navigate our way to people like us that are hiding in the Dark Web if we asked him. It could be useful to connect with them.'

They talked for over an hour. Staying connected with networks of like minded individuals prepared to think about more than just themselves had always been critical to the long term success of the *20/20 Project*. Of course, there were risks, but being careful didn't mean you couldn't also be brave.

It was Christmas Eve before everything was in place. In a very short time it had become only too obvious that Mark, John and in particular Naomi, held pivotal roles in the community. They understood immediately why it was so important to house the laptop and begin work on sharing the work of the Project.

'Who knows what knowledge will survive into the future?' said Isaac.' The powerful have always covered their tracks. There are people with a vested interest in ensuring a privileged few hold onto information.'

'It's crucial that we reach out to communities beyond those of us here though as well. People that believe as we do,' said Nick.

'It's always like this,' mused Naomi. 'Knowledge even in short supply is valuable.'

Nick looked at Isaac, recalling a conversation they'd had almost nine years before about border controls. It was incredible to him, looking back, how much had changed. Isaac had seen this whole situation coming, been alert to the impact of a growing scarcity of resources on the way people would behave.

'Isaac anticipated this. I was naive. I wanted to believe world leaders would take appropriate action while they still could.'

'It's not rocket science,' Isaac muttered. Nick viewed his brother-in-law with wary eyes. He was like a pressure cooker, waiting to explode. He reached across, placing a reassuring hand on his shoulder. Isaac shrugged it off angrily.

'No snowflake ever feels responsible for the carnage caused by the avalanche,' replied Naomi gently. Nick wished he could be more like her. Her ability to be wise, stay calm in a crisis played a huge part in holding the community together and he suspected they would be lost without her.

'True, but I've always struggled with that mentality,' said Nick. 'If we allow ourselves to have those thoughts we'll feel beaten before we even start.'

Naomi nodded.

'We can none of us change the whole world, but we can at least make a difference to the corner we've been given,' she smiled. 'We can't spend our lives blaming our parents, the government, society. At some point we have to acknowledge our own accountability for how our lives and stories turn out.'

'That's not to say we can't make mistakes-we are only human after all. I've always thought we over complicate and that it's much simpler than we make out. We just have to make the world a little better for people. That's what your Project and the Programme you've produced is all about. It's going to be the greatest Christmas present we've ever had.'

December 24th 2054

Of all the days in the year, Hope loved Christmas Eve best. The uncertainty over whether 'he' would really come, even though, deep down, she always knew he would, was a strong memory from childhood. She loved the rituals passed from her parents that like them she'd always known: the stockings at the chimney, the carrot half chewed in the morning, the empty glass by the fireplace. Even though so much had changed in their lives, some of these traditions and Christmas as an event was still something that families clung to as a time for being together.

She recalled being in her bedroom as a child, searching the skies for signs of a sledge, almost convincing herself she'd seen one. She'd gone to sleep full of anticipation that presents would be there in the morning.

And, of course, when she was small they always were; wrapped in endless crinkled paper, tied with ribbon, followed by a meal round a laden table and a day filled with games and laughter.

She and Jude had grown up sharing these times. The two families cooked and ate together over the years. There had always been closeness, a sense of being a part of something special. She hadn't realised it at the time, but looking back they had been lucky.

'So what happens at Christmas here?' she'd asked Hannah. Hope had met and become friends with Hannah in the first week on the island, delighted to get to know someone her own age who understood her need for laughter, to ask questions and share dreams. Now they were sorting through a huge pile of greenery collected from across the island to decorate the Gathering House.

Hannah continued to pick over the foliage, snipping and twisting it into long garlands that would be hung from the rafters. She'd arrived with her family the year before, having made the long journey north from London to join her grandparents, residents on the island for years. Like many families, uncertainties and concerns about what the future might hold had led to them taking a decision to move closer to each other.

'It's great, Hope, honest, you'll love it. We all bring food to share, there's music and dancing and everyone's together. Christmas here is the best.'

Hope was ready for a party. Everyone had made them feel so welcome and she couldn't believe how well they'd got to know people in the community already. But it had been hard work too and this chance to relax and have some fun felt long overdue.

Lots of people were decorating the Gathering House. The riot of ivy and evergreen was something very different from the richness of manufactured Christmas decorations of the past. Then there had been swags dripping with gold and silver ribbon, scarlet berries and shiny holly twisted to plastic perfection. The island's Christmas loveliness lay in this unmatched abundance and variegation, a natural beauty woven into magical garlands wrapped like feather boas around chairs, tables, pillars. Branches hung from rafters, suffusing the air with the perfume of damp pine.

Everything was homemade: tables set with napkins and cutlery twisted round with ivy, the centre pieces made from candles and berries. Fiddle and folk players were grouped around the stage, trying out riffs and verses of songs, some familiar, others crafted specially for the occasion.

Hope's eyes rested on the young people milling about. The youngest were barely teenagers, enjoying the opportunity to hang out with others older than they were. She remembered how much she'd loved joining conversations she couldn't have at home, the chance to mimic different styles of dress, ways of speaking, attitudes. She'd been in such a hurry to grow up. Now it seemed her childhood had passed in a flash and she was someone with responsibilities, a grown up. And she knew now that being an adult wasn't easy.

One of the musicians seemed to be drawing special interest from the younger teenagers. Pete was Hannah's older brother. At eighteen he and Hope were almost the same age and she'd noticed him almost as soon as they'd arrived. He reminded her of her father in some ways: comfortable with himself, an easy smile. His hair flopped over eyes that shone with warmth and a quiet intelligence. He was good looking, and he knew it. Hope nudged Hannah.

'Your brother's fan club's in town.'

Hannah grinned. 'Too right. Look at them. If he gets any more attention he'll be even more unbearable to live with than ever!'

Seeing the two of them looking across, Peter made his excuses, rested his guitar on its stand and strolled over. Hope busied herself with twining leaves and berries while Hannah teased her brother about his following.

'What's a guy supposed to do?' he joked. 'Can I help it if I'm so irresistible?'

Hannah swiped him with a branch of holly.

'Ow, that hurt!'

'You deserve it. You'd better be careful. Santa doesn't like bigheads.'

He pulled up a stool and wound some leaves into a crown which he dropped onto Hope's head, arching an eyebrow.

'I'd better watch out then. What are you two hoping for in your stockings?'

They worked and chatted together for most of the afternoon. By tea time the room had been transformed from meeting space to woodland fairytale. As darkness fell candles were lit in lanterns dotted around the room, casting shadows on walls and picking out features of people in all four corners. Hope didn't say much, preferring to listen to the gentle banter that flowed between Peter and Hannah, typical brother and sister teasing.

They were almost finished when she spotted Jude hovering at the door. She guessed he had been helping his father. They were always together these days working on the *20/20 Project*. She wasn't too sure what they did or what was involved but it was something to do with safeguarding its contents. She knew from overheard conversations that there was a lot of concern about viruses introduced by underground groups that might want to corrupt the files the *20/20* team had worked so hard to create. They were trying to put in firewalls so that only those people they could trust could get through. It was a tricky balance. They wanted to communicate with other communities like their own, but they didn't want someone breaking into the database and sabotaging what they'd spent so long putting together. There were people out there who'd made it their business in the past to hack into systems with sensitive data; information on national defence, individuals' health records and bank details. The list was endless. The internet was a place where it was hard to keep anything secure.

Hope waved and Jude slipped through the crowded room, stopping a few feet from the table. He was wearing a cap which he pulled off, wiping it across his brow and tossing it onto the table. Hannah jumped.

'Oh, Jude, I didn't see you.'

He muttered an apology, picked up the cap and turned around, going back the way he had come, out of the door into the dusk. Pete rolled his eyes.

'What's his problem?'

'He's been helping Isaac on the Project every single day since we got here,' Hope snapped. 'They have to work all hours. Life's not all music and dancing for them, you know.'

'Pardon me for breathing,' Pete's hands were raised in mock humiliation. Suddenly, she'd had enough of him. Making her excuses Hope followed Jude outside.

She decided to take the path down to the jetty to catch the last rays of the sun. Approaching the headland she spotted a figure silhouetted against the skyline and realised it was her cousin. Jude turned at the sound of her footsteps on the loose shale and she took his arm as they watched the waters turn to ink.

'Have you been helping on the Project again?'

Jude nodded 'There's always so much to do. Dad's panicking,'

Hope could imagine what that would be like. Her uncle could be a hard taskmaster. If he was panicking you could be sure it would be Jude he'd be taking his frustrations out on. And if he wasn't there, it would be his mother. She'd heard her parents talking and knew they hated how Isaac treated Ellie. It wasn't as if he hit her, but what he did do was just as damaging. She was scared of him, seemed to plead with her eyes when they were together, not wanting to make a scene, but still trying to make things better between them. She could tell Jude hated seeing his mother cowed like that.

'You look tired.'

Jude shrugged. 'I'm OK.'

They sat for a few more minutes, Hope had got her cousin nothing for Christmas and willed herself to say something that would comfort him and connect them, bring them closer together as they had been as children. In the end she blurted out:

'Pete's an idiot sometimes.'

Jude said nothing, lent forward, elbows on knees, running his fingers through his hair and down the sides of his face.

'Are you OK Jude?'

He muttered something she didn't catch.

'Sorry, what did you say?'

Without looking at her, he stood and strode back along the path. Scurrying after him, Hope reached out and grabbed his arm.

'What Jude? What's up?'

He stopped in his tracks, shoving her hand away with such passion that she was almost knocked off balance. In the gloom she made out the outline of his sharp features but not the detail. Stepping forward, she was shocked to see his eyes were glistening with tears.

Not daring to touch him, Hope crossed her arms, clenching her hands into tight, frustrated fists. He was like a wild creature, ready to bolt at the slightest provocation. Pete's comments wouldn't have helped, but she suspected this outburst had more to do with Jude spending a day under Isaac's critical gaze. He could be such a shit. In the face of her uncle's taunts she knew she wouldn't be able to stay silent, but Jude was different. He kept his feelings corked up; no wonder he exploded from time to time. In some ways she preferred those outbursts to their alternative. At least they were something she could get a grip on.

Sensing he was struggling to regain control of his emotions she waited for him to speak, at the same time edging closer till their arms were almost touching.

'Pete's a prat,' he muttered.

She wasn't going to contradict him in this mood. Jude turned towards the village and they made the short walk back in silence.

As they approached the square the sound of voices, first muffled and then becoming more recognisable floated through the darkness. The preparations for the evening's entertainment were coming to a climax. Jude stopped dead and slipped into the shadows cast by the gated archway at the entrance to the church.

'Will you come to the party?' asked Hope. 'It's a chance to get out, see everyone. It might help.'

Snorting with derision, Jude pushed open the gate and headed into the churchyard. Wending his way through the lichen covered crosses and the assorted memorials he reached a huge yew tree that had witnessed generations of remembrances. Hope followed, picking her way over the pitted track and crouched next to him.

'I'm not coming.'

'Why?' she asked.

'Because I'm not, OK? The last thing I feel like doing is hanging out with people pretending.'

'Pretending what?'

'That we're one big happy family. That the world's a great place. That we're all glad to be alive.'

'I am glad to be alive. I know it's not perfect here, but we've got food, shelter, friendship. It feels a whole lot safer than where we were.'

Jude's tone was withering. 'You don't get it do you? Do you honestly think we're safe here?'

'Well, I know there's danger, obviously, and none of us can know the future. But, yes, I feel safe, a part of something. I've got a place, a purpose.'

Jude rested his head against the trunk.

'You're nuts.'

'Charming.'

'Being here doesn't mean safety and freedom. If anything it means more duty, more responsibility.'

He sounded so like Isaac when he was, as she'd heard her father describe it, 'having a rant' that Hope had to stifle the urge to giggle.

'Surely one night off's not going to matter? You're exhausted, you need a break. The party will give you something else to think about for once. I'm worried about you Jude; your dad's working you too hard. I want you to come.'

He remained where he was. Throwing caution to the wind, Hope decided to sit down and rest her head alongside his, against the tree. She'd expected him to flinch away, but to her relief he didn't. They stared into the countless pinpricks of light forming swirls like twinkling gossamer above them. The more she looked the more her eyes became accustomed to the darkness and she felt drawn into a vastness of space that went on and on, extraordinary and awesome in a universe that was itself miraculous and unfathomable. She had a sense of drowning, of tumbling head over heels into the darkness.

Her grandmother had once said 'We all need an anchor, something or someone we can turn to and trust.' Hope wanted to communicate this permission to reach out to people to Jude and unlock a capacity to love and be loved. She wanted him to feel safe too.

Hope looked at her cousin in the darkness.

'It's Christmas, Jude. I wish I could give you something, help you believe in the future like I do.'

Jude sighed. 'You've tried, Hope,' he said and getting to his feet, he strode away without her.

******   ******   ******

The Gathering House was alive with laughter. Long tables, for once filled with fruits and vegetables, meats and morsels prepared with all the care and attention one might give to a feast for gods, greeted them. Steaming broths laced with sweet rosemary and oozing rich creamy sauce were being ladled out and mopped up with hunks of freshly baked crusty bread. Platters were passed from one to the other, food piled unusually high.

And there was wine, brewed and bottled from berries gathered from hedgerows, fermented and crafted in kitchen cauldrons till they became the deepest reds, purest whites and freshest pinks. Concocting such brews from the basest of materials required mastery akin to magic. The liquids would become dream makers, love potions, weaving their wonder and turning, for one night only, paupers into princes.

When she eventually returned, Hope spotted Pete as soon as she walked in. He was standing to one side, clutching a jug and two mugs, scanning the room. The moment he saw her he headed across, handed her a mug and filled it with hot wine.

'I've been watching for you. I'm sorry about earlier. Didn't mean to be an arse. Forgive me?'

She nodded and they chinked their mugs together. The liquid danced like fire in her throat, heat chasing all the way through her. She had never tasted anything as delicious.

'Have you eaten yet?'

'No, just arrived. I was looking for Jude.'

'He's over here, he just beat you back. Come on, we've saved you a seat.' And placing one hand on her shoulder he steered her through the crowds to a trestle where Hannah, Jude and some of the other young people were already feasting. Hope slipped in next to her cousin, giving him a swift hug.

'I thought I wasn't going to see you. I'm so glad you came.'

He leant towards her and put his mouth to her ear so only she would hear.

'Thanks, Hope. I'm sorry about before. I'm just so tired. Happy Christmas.'

He rested his shoulder on hers and she reached up and kissed him gently on the cheek. Already flushed with wine, he went even redder and looked away. She felt so sorry for him. After all he was just lonely, and for all his aloofness, probably a little bit scared. Remembering a line from a film they used to watch together as children she squeezed his hand.

'I see you, Jude.'

'I see you too, Hope.'

Pete stretched across the table with the hot wine to refill everyone's cups and then shuffled onto the bench on the other side of her.

'Come on everyone, let's eat!'

It was an unforgettable evening. Once the food was finished, the tables were taken down or pushed to the edge of the room and the floor cleared for dancing. Pete and the other musicians took to the stage and reel after reel was beaten out on bodrums accompanied by their nimble fingers flying over fiddles, accordion and whistles. Music tumbled like a waterfall from the instruments in joyful harmonies.

Hope danced every chance she had, and when she wasn't dancing she drank and laughed, revelling in the sense of belonging. She watched as Nick swept Eva up and twirled her round as one tune ended. He wrapped her in his arms and held her close.

There was a time when she'd have been horrified if she had caught her parents kissing, would have squirmed with disapproval and embarrassment. Now it gave her a warm glow to see them. She had sometimes wondered why their love for each other should make her so content. Tonight she understood. It freed her. They loved Hope, of course, but they also loved each other. Hope could follow her own heart and they would follow theirs.

Jude's parents were sat together, barely communicating. Hope sensed that Ellie wanted to dance, but it was awkward to step into the imaginary exclusion zone that seemed to have formed around them. Nick danced with Ellie a couple of times and Eva was her usual self, chatting and trying to draw Isaac into conversation. But it was clear that if you weren't family you wouldn't bother. Isaac's face registered boredom, disapproval and growing irritation. His fingers drummed on the table as he sipped on the wine in his cup. There were too many awkward silences between Isaac and Ellie and other more entertaining distractions for people to make the additional effort needed to break through the cold front that pervaded the atmosphere around the pair of them.

    She wondered if Jude had noticed the awkwardness but was reassured to see that, for once, he appeared more taken up with the conversations of the young people around him. He had danced with her twice, and on each occasion she had tried her best to give him her full attention. She wanted to make him feel special.

    The wine was weaving its spell and loosening tongues and reserve. One of the young women, Beth, had taken the seat next to Jude while Hope had been dancing with Pete who was having a break from playing. She was sat, staring up at Jude with dark eyes and it didn't look like she was going to move. Pete pulled Hope towards him and, nodding at the two of them, winked.

    'Shall we get some air?'

    Grabbing her wine she let him lead her around the edge of the whirling dancers to the back of the room where they rested their weight against the metal bar that kept the exit door closed. The wood had swollen in the damp end of year air. They both pushed with their shoulders till it flew open and they half fell out into the darkness, stumbling into each other and giggling with wine induced laughter, resting against the walls of the porch.

'It's freezing out here,' moaned Hope.

Pete wrapped his arms around her.

'Watch out, you're spilling my wine,' she giggled, laughing up into his eyes.

What happened next was probably inevitable, but so unexpected she later wondered if it had been a dream. Everything went still. Pete took the mug from her hand, setting it on the ledge that ran round the inside of the sheltering walls.

The wine, the music and Christmas Eve were a heady mix, the moment froze in the moonlight and she was beautiful. Their eyes locked in mute realisation of the spark between them and closed as their lips met.

They stayed outside, wrapped together till they were so cold they had to go back in. As they opened the door they were met by a wave of noise that enveloped them and drew them once again back into the festivities. Hope, very aware that her parents were in all likelihood wondering where she'd been, kept her eyes down as they returned to the table. Beth was still in her seat but there was no sign of Jude or his parents. Hannah cocked an eyebrow in Hope's direction, gulping down her wine and the two girls giggled helplessly as Pete shrugged his shoulders at his sister with mock nonchalance. He stood behind Hope and aware of his presence she didn't look round until he rested a hand on her shoulder, bent down and whispered in her ear.

'OK?'

She smiled up at him over her shoulder.

'Very.'

The room had become soft focused and the lights and sound to Hope were fuzzy at the edges. Voices washed over her in waves and she felt that if she were to close her eyes she would slip into sleep. It was time to go home.

She nudged Hannah and the pair began a round of hugs and goodbyes. When she got to Pete he pulled her close and she nestled into his chest. It would have been so easy to stay there.....

'Think I'll take over from here.' Nick was at her side, wrapping protective fatherly arms around her. Eva helped her on with her coat and all three of them made their way through the hall to the front door, offering their goodbyes and good wishes to everyone.

The cottage was nearby. Hope had no memory of the journey but she made it to her room, tugged off her shoes and clothes and dropped them where they landed, falling almost naked into bed, loving the feel of the cotton against her skin. She gave herself over to Christmas dreams, fingers reaching up to touch her hair and lips until, in her sleep, something made her smile.

Six Years Later

October 31st 2060

The door of the cottage bounced on its hinges as it slammed shut.

'That is it.'

Eva came running down stairs.

'What the hell's going on?'

Nick was pacing round the room, breathing hard.

'It's Isaac. He's wanting to introduce a no work, no food rule.'

'What?'

Nick threw himself into a chair.

'He doesn't think it's fair if members of the Community who aren't working get food.'

Eva took a moment to process what she'd heard. Over the years Nick had been bringing home reports of Isaac's increasingly bizarre declarations. But this was one of the more outrageous.

'What does he mean, not working? Is he thinking about people taking time out because they're old or ill? He surely doesn't expect them to go out and plough a field does he?'

Nick glanced up. Eva thought he looked tired. He was still handsome, but he'd never stopped working and sometimes she forgot they weren't getting any younger.

'I don't know love. But to be honest, if he had his way I think he'd have all of us out there slaving till we drop. He thinks we're being overrun by wasters. That we're making excuses and some people are getting away with not doing their fair share.'

'Don't know where he gets that idea from! I end up exhausted most days.'

'He's not talking about us. We're the good guys as far as he's concerned. It's people he judges are spongers.'

'That's ridiculous. We all do what we can. Not everyone can dig, not everyone can cook. And even if you could, sometimes you just don't feel up to it.'

Nick sat back in the chair.

'Don't let Isaac hear you say that. He's got no time for feelings.'

Eva had always known that. To be honest she'd never been able to understand what Ellie had seen in her brother. They were very different. Timing had probably played a part in them getting together. When they'd first met Ellie had been on the rebound from a long relationship. She'd been vulnerable, Isaac needy. They'd gone out often as a foursome and always had fun. Being together had clouded the differences between them, changed the dynamics.

It was only when Ellie and Isaac were married, and then when Jude had come along that the strain had really started to show. Unlike Hope, who seemed to sail through her early years, Jude had lurched from one illness to another, often not sleeping or feeling unwell, leaving his parents exhausted.

'Our Isaac's not good at sharing is he? It's almost like he resents Jude being there,' Eva had once commented to Nick after the four of them had double dated and her brother had spent the whole evening dismissing any conversations about the children in favour of talk of his work on the Project.

'He's been such a sickly baby. Maybe Isaac's afraid there's something wrong with him, that's why he holds back?' her husband had speculated. 'Do you think having Jude has changed Ellie?'

'She's a mother for goodness sake. Of course she's changed. Isaac's just a selfish git.' muttered Eva. 'He always was a control freak.'

She had never been a fan of the way Isaac spoke to Ellie and had tried in vain in the early days of their courtship to put some distance between the two of them or at least encourage Ellie to stand up for herself. She'd tried broaching the subject with her brother once and been well and truly put in her little sister place.

'Sometimes you talk down to Ellie, you know. She doesn't say anything but she gets upset, I can tell.'

Isaac had shrugged his shoulders.

'She knows I don't mean it. And anyway, it's not really any of your business how we talk to each other, so butt out. You won't hear me commenting on yours and Nick's relationship, even though I think the pair of you act like a couple of big kids most of the time.'

That was her told.

Isaac was her brother. He had worked with Nick for years. She had come to accept that while she might not always like him, she loved Isaac. Their lives were tangled together.

Nick was such a different father. He'd seen Hope as a gift, precious as a daughter to him but also as a granddaughter to his parents because she stood partly in the place his younger sister Mia had left when she had died as a baby. It wasn't Jude's fault that he'd been a sickly child. He hadn't asked to be born. Looking back, she had always felt sorry for her nephew.

'So what's given Isaac this latest idea?'

Nick sighed. 'He's just looking at the practicalities. The trouble is that, in his mind, the balance here now is all wrong. When Naomi was in charge when we first arrived she gave a particular steer based on her values. But Isaac thinks it was simply that back then the islanders could afford to be welcoming. Now he feels we've got back to the situation we had in the village with too many people consuming resources and not enough producing any. As far as he's concerned it is history repeating itself and that makes him anxious. And, to be fair, he's not alone.'

'That's one way of putting it. He can be very persuasive. You could say he's panicking because he thinks he has to be in control and that it's his job to sort everything out. He learned to do that when he was a kid.'

Isaac had been a teenager when his and Eva's father had run out on the family, with the excuse that he was too young to be a father. Isaac had been expected to shoulder the responsibility of being the man of the house for their mother and he'd also acted as Eva's childhood protector.

'It's what Isaac's done since Dad left us. He has to be the responsible one, planning ahead, anticipating problems. To be honest, I don't know how he sleeps.'

'I don't think he does. One of the team was telling me he wakes up most nights and sees him from his bathroom window walking on the beach.'

'Well if he's not getting sleep that can't be helping him to think clearly. Should I try and talk to him? I'm not saying I'll do any better than you, but he might find it easier to tell me what's going on in his head.'

Nick appeared about to answer when, for the second time the door of the cottage was slammed shut. This time it was Hope who flew into the room. She pulled off her hat, scarf, coat and gloves, flinging them to the floor.

'Bloody Uncle Isaac! You'll never guess what he's done now.'

Eva slid off Nick's knee.

'What?'

Hope pulled a paper from a pocket.

'He's called a meeting of the whole Community to reallocate duties.'

Nick took the notice from her hand.

'Where did you find this?'

'They're all round the village. I found Jude pinning them up.'

'Nothing's been brought to the Council. This isn't the way things are done around here.'

Hope rolled her eyes.

'Dad, not being funny, but when was there ever a time that Uncle Isaac took any notice of *how things get done around here?* He's a complete law unto himself. He just sees the Council as a talking shop, a waste of time. If he wants something to happen and he believes he's right, he won't care what the Council thinks. He'll just do it.'

Her parents looked shocked, but she could tell they knew she was right. She'd overheard them talking a few times about her uncle and had walked in on a couple of occasions when Isaac and her father appeared to be having 'words.' A confrontation had been brewing for a while.

'No one'll turn up,' said Eva. 'They'll know this isn't authorised by the Council and they'll just boycott the meeting.'

Hope flung a withering look in her direction.

'Mum, honestly, you can be so naive sometimes. Isaac's not the kind of person that sticks up a few posters on a whim and hopes for the best. He'll have been plotting this for months. Surely you've picked up on the change in atmosphere since Naomi died? She was the only one who could control him. She had the loyalty and respect of the Community, people listened to her. Now she's gone there's no one he feels he has to take any notice of, especially not the Council.'

Naomi's death a few months before had been traumatic for everyone, especially Nick. It hadn't been unexpected, but as the last survivor of the old order, she had held everyone's respect and been critical to helping them all feel they belonged. Without her presence the Community had lost its leader and felt rudderless.

Isaac had responded the quickest to the vacuum, setting aside any sense of loss and seizing the opportunity to build a platform for himself.

Hope rested her eyes on her parents as they huddled on the faded, threadbare settee. It was a while since she'd really looked at them. They looked smaller somehow. When had they grown so old?

Tonight was going to be interesting.

****** ****** ******

The evening was dank with sleeting rain and a raw biting wind blowing from the north. Figures making their way to the Gathering House were indistinguishable from each other, moving like conspirators in heavy hoods cloaking identities. They loomed out of the darkness, footsteps ringing on the sharp, uneven surfaces of slate and stone around the building.

Inside it was cold. There hadn't been time to make up fires and, in any case, kindling was scarce. People pulled out chairs and scattered in haphazard groups, some standing, resting against walls, others flopping to the floor or perching on tables and window ledges. The atmosphere was tense, restless; no one wanted to draw attention to themselves.

Pete met Hope just outside the entrance. On either side of the door lurked several large men blocking the way, turning a few people away and waving others through. Once inside, they made their way to the front of the room. Nick and Eva were already there, speaking to members of the Council gathering around them. They were trying to behave naturally, nodding greetings, enquiring into the latest news of different families, taking a hand here, wrapping an arm round a shoulder there. But Hope registered a gaze not quite met, a cheek turned away. They might all be a part of the same story, but they were no longer on the same page.

She searched the crowd, noting that everyone there was a long standing resident. She tried to find her Aunt Ellie, but instead spotted Jude. She barely saw him these days as he was always with his father. Uncle Isaac was speaking to him with intent and Jude was giving his full attention, nodding and making notes in a book which he then slipped into his back pocket. Making his way to a dark corner, half shielded by the thick curtain at the window, he took out the notebook and scanning the crowd, continued to scribble.

Jude saw Hope watching and she raised her hand in greeting. She was certain he must have seen her but he did not respond. Instead his eyes ferreted through the gathering audience.

Isaac mounted the stage and everyone fell silent. He walked to the centre, gripped the lectern and, in that instant, took control. Suddenly, and from nowhere, Hope felt a lump in her throat and reached for Pete's hand. He squeezed it tight and leant towards her, a comforting presence. She almost cried.

'Greetings neighbours. I acknowledge that this meeting has been called at short notice and,' he nodded towards Nick, 'without permissions from the Council. However, we have long had a tradition of free speech in this Community and a belief in personal as well as collective responsibility. It is these traditions that have driven me to bring you together tonight.'

Hope looked across to Nick. He sat in silence, arms folded across his chest, eyes fixed on Isaac. Eva was sitting bolt upright, gripping her chair.

Isaac continued.

'In the last few weeks many of you have spoken to me about your concerns for our Community. In recent times we have seen a number of strangers join us. In many cases they are escaping hardships drawn by the advantages that our Community offers, the benefits and privileges we have established through hard work, careful stewardship and toil.'

'These incomers have not earned these benefits and many do not contribute to creating them. Is that fair? Is that right?'

A grumbling murmur rumbled round the room. Hope felt Pete's grip tighten.

'Sometimes I walk through our Community and find I barely know the names of some that I pass. New arrivals whose way of life, clothes, religion, even language differs from our own.'

'How do we want to care for our families? What kind of Community do we want to leave to our grandchildren? And how do we set about making sure that we achieve that? How do we choose between those that contribute and those that do not? And who should make those decisions now Naomi has so sadly died? Should it be the Council or someone else?'

'One family, you will know who I mean, think nothing of piling their filthy rubbish in the yard where they live. It should not be necessary to explain why this is unacceptable, it should be obvious. But, reassured by our tolerance, they ignore their responsibilities to the Community. They take us for fools.'

Hope whispered to Pete.

'He's talking about the Shampalis. They've been traumatised by everything that happened to them before they came here. They barely know what day of the week it is. He's making them sound like complete wasters.'

Isaac had warmed to his theme. 'We know the problems others face. Our remoteness is our salvation but it also makes us attractive to those seeking a way out of their dilemmas. The risk is that we become overrun. Like many of you, I fear for the continuation of our Community, our shared identity, our culture, our way of life.'

One of the Council raised a hand to speak. It was Flora, Pete's mother. She got to her feet. Tall and slim, she appeared patient, cautious, standing as still as a heron waiting to spear its prey. She'd lived on the island most of her early life, and was attuned to its vagaries, having an uncanny knack of being able to read and predict the weather from her observations of tiny changes in the sea and the sky. Over the time Hope and Pete had been together Flora had passed on much of her knowledge to Hope who, as a result, had developed a keen eye for reading and interpreting events in the natural world.

Irritated by the interruption, Isaac glowered but then appeared to remember himself and gathered his emotions tight, wrapping and hiding them under hooded eyes and a twisted smile. He waved Flora forward. Ignoring the gesture, she stepped instead up onto her chair and from there to the table around which she and the other Council members were gathered. She planted her feet and, turning to the audience, drew herself erect. A silver slide holding her mane of raven black hair away from her face glinted in the candle light and a grey skirt, belted tunic and heavy cloak cascaded around her like robes. She looked magnificent.

There was some shuffling and muttering in the audience. Flora waited for silence.

When the room was still she reached over her shoulder and pulled forward a fiddle hanging by a strap on her back, nestling it under her chin. The bow was sheathed at her waist. In a single movement that flowed from her fingers to her arm and along to her fingers again she began to slide the bow back and forward across the strings.

The melody that emerged was haunting, exquisite. Everyone recognised the tune; the words ran through the minds of the listeners, each associating them with events where they had been sung. They had passed down through generations of islanders and in turn been shared with new settlers. The song spoke of families and friends bound together through shared humanity, adversity and love. It was a song for weddings and funerals, new births, old deaths; every human experience, each transition, every memory.

She finished with a long draw across the strings and stood, head bowed, fiddle and bow hanging from hands dropped to either side of her body as if the music had stirred, unsettled but in a strange way reunited them so now no one quite knew what to do.

Isaac looked furious but it was Nick who broke the silence. He got to his feet and helped his fellow Council member down from the table.

'Thank you Flora. That was beautiful. To remember songs we have shared is to remember memories we have made, to tighten the bonds between us.'

'As Isaac has outlined, we have a challenge. Throughout history human beings have engaged with or avoided people different from themselves, built walls or negotiated alliances, become curious and attracted to new arrivals or run away from them in fear.'

Nick paused.

'One might say that the attempt to live a peaceful life in a community made up of people with differences is what marks out and epitomises civilisation.'

He turned towards Isaac, who was watching him like a hawk, and smiled.

'You have heard what my friend Isaac has to say. I respect him, but it is obvious that he and I see our responsibilities here very differently. While ever we can, I intend to continue to find ways to welcome all people regardless of colour, creed, age or disability into our Community as one brother and sisterhood. Naive, perhaps, but compassion and tolerance, I believe, need to be at the heart of how we live.'

'Isaac does not agree with me, and I sense that some of you wish to follow his lead. That is your right, your choice and prerogative. I have nothing more to say on the subject, we are each answerable for our own actions. Love can accommodate difference, it always has. The question is: can our Community?'

And with that, Nick reached out his hand to Eva. She stood and, without a backward glance they made their way out of the hall and into whatever future awaited them.

November 1st 2060

Hope hadn't slept. She and Pete sat up turning over what had been said at the meeting. Once Nick and Eva had left no one else had seemed either willing or to have the heart to speak and not long afterwards the gathering had broken up. Families had drifted out into the darkness to continue their discussions, behind closed doors. She and Pete had gone to his parents' cottage.

'This isn't going to go away is it?'

Pete had wrapped his arms round her shoulders, planting a kiss on the crown of her head and resting his cheek there. They were stretched out on the sofa, watching the dying embers of the fire in its wide hearth. Flora and Jim had gone to bed long before, claiming tiredness, but in reality wanting time to talk. There was a sense of resignation but also a new determination in both of them. The whole evening had felt like a watershed.

'I'd give anything to be a fly on the wall at Isaac's tonight,' Pete murmured as they kissed good night. 'Do you think he saw your dad's speech coming?'

Hope continued to stare into the fire.

'Probably. They've been friends for such a long time. They know each other pretty well. Were you surprised?'

'Not really. Your dad's always been one to pick his battles. He has his beliefs, but he'd never force them on anyone else. He lets people find their own way.'

Hope nodded slowly. 'You're right, they feel responsible. They've got their values and they've made no secret of those all my life. I haven't always agreed with them, but I've probably soaked them up over the years.'

'I know. They'll always take the road that's less travelled. What matters to them is to treat everyone the same. And if that brings challenges and difficulties, so be it.'

'Dad always taught me we have a duty to try and walk in the other person's shoes, find out what makes them act the way they do. It's not always easy to feel love for someone that's different. But when you do, it ignites you. It's like fuel. He used to tell me that really loving someone, especially someone you didn't know or understand, took more discipline and effort than giving out judgements or criticism or hatred.'

'I guess it opens the door to new possibilities.'

'But he also used to tell me that love was a muscle and you have to exercise it to make it strong.'

The next morning father and daughter were perched side by side on tussocks nestled in dunes that stretched along the shoreline. From this vantage point they could look down onto a quiet sea, glittering like a sheet of diamonds in the early sunshine. They were sheltered from the breeze which played around them, tugging at Hope's scarf and Nick's jacket. It was the sort of morning they both loved, full of promise, when the island was at its most beautiful and ignoring human realities, appeared content.

'This is not a choice we can make for you, my love. The final decision has to be yours.'

Sitting beside her father, looking across the vastness of the sea, Hope scooped up a small piece of beach and allowed the grains of sand to trickle through her fingers, wondering if the tininess of her existence even mattered.

And in that moment she made the decision that would change her life forever.

November 5th 2060

It was far easier than Hope had expected to persuade Pete. Was this a sign of what they had come to mean to each other she wondered?

'If this hadn't happened I'd have been thinking about leaving anyway,' he said. 'And where ever you go, I'm coming too. There's a place further north I've been in touch with through the Project. I think we could fit in there.'

Hope was relieved that some positive contact had been made with what she thought of as the outside world.

'You never quite know who you can trust. A hacker could be screening any communication trying to find out something they could sell.'

'We can't afford to let our guard down,' she'd heard her father saying to Isaac as she'd drifted in on them in their kitchen one night after work.

'Don't worry, we've some good people on the Team now, Neil's been invaluable passing on his security knowledge, Pete's getting up to speed and Jude's got a really tight hold on managing the risks.' Isaac broke off as Hope came into the room.

'Oh, hello, didn't see you there. How's it going?'

They'd chatted for a short time but Hope had sensed she was interrupting and making her excuses had gone to bed. It was almost an hour later that she'd heard the back door click shut and her father making his way slowly upstairs to bed.

Hope had been seeing less and less of Jude as time went on. They were busy with different aspects of life on the island. She seemed always out in the fields, weeding gardens or tending livestock. Jude spent much of his time indoors, either in the crypt or shadowing his father. He was never without the notebook. She'd not managed to look inside properly but she could see that each page was covered with his close handwriting, line after line of details, names and dates and lists of actions that he ticked off methodically.

'Each to their own,' she'd once commented to Pete. 'Whatever Jude's doing for the Project, I'm pretty sure Isaac's checking up on him.'

She and Pete had been growing closer with each month that passed. They didn't spend much time together alone as there always seemed so much to do, others to support. But when they did manage to snatch a moment it was as if they'd not been apart. Hope found herself saving stories and thoughts that she might once have shared with her father so she could instead bring them to him first. It wasn't that she didn't still talk to the other girls, or turn to her parents. But one day she realised that without her noticing, Pete had somehow become her best friend.

Hannah had spoken to her about it earlier in the summer. She and Hope were picking the first crop of raspberries from canes they'd been tending.

'You do realise my brother's smitten don't you Hope?' she'd giggled.

Hope had concentrated on reaching some particularly awkward berries just out of reach and tried not to blush.

'How do you mean, smitten?'

'Come on, you must have seen the way he looks at you. He practically drools!'

Hope climbed down from the upturned crate, dropped her basket and flopped to the ground. Hannah helped herself to a small handful of the fruit, savouring the rich sweetness of their juice.

'Do you really think he likes me?'

Hannah snorted. 'Mad for you! Do you fancy him?'

An image of Pete's warm brown eyes and his smile as he pushed a tangle of dark curls away from his forehead flashed before her imagination. Yes, she thought it was safe to say she fancied him.

'He wasn't too happy when you got partnered up with that Andrew Mitchell for night fishing last week,' Hannah giggled. 'He had a feeling that was Jude's idea.'

Hope blinked in amazement. 'You're kidding? I can't imagine Jude's even aware there is such a thing as night fishing. And your brother's certainly got nothing to worry about as far as Andrew's concerned. He's crazy about Amy. Never stopped talking about her the whole time we were out.'

'I know, I told Pete that, but he wasn't having it. I think he was just wishing he'd had that chance to spend time with you alone.'

Hope sighed. 'To be honest, I'd have liked that too.'

Hannah jumped up and did a little jig on the spot.

'I knew it! I knew it. You do like him!'

Hope lay back in the grass and let the warmth of the sunshine soak into her skin.

'Guilty as charged,' she giggled and the pair lay where they were, sharing secrets and longings till the heat of the day was over and the shadows were starting to lengthen.

'It's getting late, we'd better get back,' said Hope. 'They'll be wondering what's happened to us.'

They had stowed the crates next to the orchard wall and, gathering up the baskets of fruit, they made their way arm in arm back down the hillside to the village. When they were almost home Hope stopped.

'Thanks Hannah,' she said.

'Thanks for what?'

'For listening to me witter on about your brother all afternoon.'

'Don't be daft. You can witter all you like. That's what friends are for.'

'You won't say anything to him, will you? I'd be mortified if he thought we'd been talking about him like this.'

Hannah rolled her eyes. 'Of course not. I'll not say a word unless you want me to. But Hope,' and she squeezed her hand ' I know he's my brother, so I'm bound to be a bit biased, but he's a good lad and I know he cares for you. A lot.'

And with that they had parted, each carrying home fruit to be turned into jams and pies by willing hands.

Hope knew she was lucky to have not just a friend in Hannah but a soul mate in her brother. Whatever the future held for them all, she was starting to believe that she and Pete would be together. And as she dwelt on that thought she felt her heart start to beat a little faster.

June 1st 2061

There were no big speeches and no dramas. It just became known that some in the Community were going to move on.

As Pete had predicted, the decision about where they would go came from the Project.

'There have always been people that rejected the sort of consumerism that drove much of how the world used resources in the past,' Nick explained. 'They were regarded by some as New Age hippies, free spirits. They drew strength from belief in the sanctity of all life. Of course, they attracted a wide range of colourful characters, determined to put the knowledge they had into simpler, smarter and more ecological living.'

One of these villages was nestled on a peninsula around two days by boat north of the island. It welcomed those that wanted to live in harmony with their surroundings and as a result an eclectic mix of people loosely bound by common values and ideals had settled there. The *20/20 Project* had been in regular contact.

The easiest route to what would become their new home was by sea. A date was fixed. All that was needed was for people to say if they wanted to go. Nick, clear from the start that this was where he was heading, had many conversations with friends and neighbours, as did Eva.

'What do you say to them Dad?' Hope asked one evening as they were preparing dinner together.

'I just say I don't claim to have rights that entitle me to snatch more than my fair share.'

'And do they agree with you or do they challenge you back?'

'It's a mixture. Of course, people raise the issue of how we can balance the needs of the few with those of the many, just like Isaac did at the meeting in October. It's not going to be easy to care for everyone, especially when the balance tips too much in one direction. But I repeat what I've said before. If we don't dare to do the right thing not just for people like 'us' but for anybody that needs a helping hand, and live, or die, with the consequences, then what are we? Civilised? I don't think so.'

He lifted the pan of vegetables they had peeled over to the stove.

'Deeds, not words, Hope, deeds not words.'

'Who do you think will come with us in the end?'

Nick was looking out of the window towards the sea. His tall, slim frame was a dark shadow that filled the space and blocked the last of the light from the setting sun. He spread his hands, his chin resting on his chest.

'I really don't know, Hope. I don't think it will be many.'

He turned to face his daughter and leaning back on the ledge, shoved his hands into the pockets of his jeans.

'My sense is there's a lot of soul searching taking place. People know the score. I wouldn't be surprised if there are some members of this Community who are coming to terms with the idea of a certain level of self sacrifice.'

'What do you mean?'

Nick crossed to the chair by the fire.

'We all have our chance with life, Hope. Some of us are lucky with the cards we're dealt and are able to live long and stay healthy, others are not so fortunate. But however life has panned out, one day our turn's over.'

She could hear the sound of the waves in the background drifting up from the shoreline, rolling forward and falling back into the sea, over and over again, timeless, eternal.

'I think some people are wondering whether it's right for them to come with us or time to step aside.'

'I don't understand. Step aside from what?'

With a sigh, Nick went back to the window and picked up a plant growing in a row with other herbs. He held it out to Hope.

'Do you know what this is?'

She took in the fern like leaves and tiny white flowers, but it was the smell of aniseed when she crushed a leaf between her finger and thumb that confirmed the plant's identity.

'It's sweet cicely.'

Nick nodded. 'And why did you check the smell?'

'Because it's so like hemlock. Everyone knows that.'

'It's one of the first lessons we learn as foragers. So explain this to me. Yesterday I came across a group of six of the oldest people on the island walking back from the burn in the woods. They each had a whole basket load of hemlock.'

June 24th 2061

They set the table in the garden, under the trees, lit with candles that bobbed in the warm summer air.

'Reminds me of when Jude and I were kids,' Hope commented to her mother. 'Decorating pies with pastry leaves and dipping our fingers into bowls of cake mix. They were good times. Perhaps it's just as well we couldn't see what was coming.'

Around seven o'clock Isaac arrived with Ellie and Jude and everyone made their way to the kitchen for drinks and conversation. Anyone watching would have seen a family enjoying time together, swapping stories, tasting and testing dishes as they came out of the oven and were carried one by one to the table bedecked with summer blooms and berries gathered from the hedgerows. There was nothing to suggest that this would be a momentous occasion that would live on in all of their memories.

Hope had garlanded each napkin with ivy twisted into rings and interlaced buttercups so that the whole picture was green and gold. She stepped back to admire her handiwork.

Making her way into the kitchen she paused at the door to take in the scene. It was a picture of a well oiled machine, individual members turning their hand to whatever they did best. Not every family could work so well together and she smiled at what she saw.

Ellie was filling jugs with herb scented water and she crossed to help.

'I feel like I've hardly seen you,' she said. 'It's been so busy getting everything ready. I can't believe this is our last night together.'

Her aunt hugged her tight. 'I'm going to miss you so much, Hope. Don't forget me will you?'

They stood together for what felt like an eternity and, when they parted, both sniffed hard and wiped their eyes with the backs of their sleeves. Ellie tried to smile.

'Look at me, what a fool. You'll be fine, we all will. I'm just being daft.'

Nick had seen the exchange and came across. He also hugged his sister.

'I wish you were coming. I can't help it. I'll always worry about you.'

Ellie looked away and busied herself with the water. Isaac sidled over. Hope and Pete had been trying to work out his thoughts for some time. Was he feeling triumphant? After all in the end he probably felt he'd won. The man with whom he had most disagreed was going.

They knew that several of the islanders who had decided their useful lives had come to an end had, in spite of every effort Nick had made to persuade them to leave with him, instead been to see Isaac about arrangements for their own deaths, claiming that this was their choice. Hope had been horrified.

'I wouldn't be surprised if Isaac gives Jude the job of taking those plans forward,' Pete had mused. 'And one day I bet he will.'

Whatever he felt, Isaac was acting with good grace tonight. Jude, for once with no notebook in sight, was making himself useful fetching and carrying. Hope caught a glance that he gave his father and Isaac gave the briefest of nods as if to say he approved. It happened in an instant, no one else would have noticed.'

Pete had seen more of Jude than she had in recent months.

'It'll be interesting to know how Jude and Aunt Ellie will react to Uncle Isaac when we're gone,' Hope said one day.

'Jude's tougher than you might imagine. He may not openly defy his father but he has other ways of challenging Isaac that are more subtle. And he's protective of his mother but you can tell she tries to keep the peace. It must be a huge strain; it's so obvious she often doesn't agree with Isaac. I feel sorry for her, but at the same time I can't understand why she puts up with him. She acts like a victim. Why doesn't she just leave?'

Hope had turned the question over in her mind for a few minutes before answering.

'I find it difficult to put myself in Ellie's shoes. She's kind and generous, if anything almost too loyal. She always puts the needs of others before her own. She believes Isaac needs her. I'm not so sure he isn't just using her. It's difficult to see what she gets out of the relationship. Maybe for her it's just better the devil she knows.'

The meal was ready. They were twelve altogether: Nick, Eva and Hope, Pete and his parents and sister, Isaac, Ellie and Jude. Abe and Sarai sat together on straight backed chairs with arms that they could grip to help them to stand. They oohed and aahed at the decorations and the meal. Food was served, glasses filled.

When it was clear that everyone had eaten as much as they wanted, there was a lull in the conversation. Nick caught Eva's eye and both stood. Silence descended.

'Thank you everyone for coming tonight. I have no intention of making a speech, but we do just want to say a few words.'

'We will miss you so much,' breathed Eva looking at Ellie. Her voice cracked with emotion.

Nick took a moment to gather himself.

'It would be convenient if life did not throw challenges our way from time to time. But then that would leave us without the opportunity to learn. The decision to leave has not been an easy one. But though after tonight we will not see each other face to face, we will think of you every day and' he also looked directly at his sister 'always love you.'

He raised his glass.

'To us all.'

Everyone stood and drank to Nick's toast.

They sat and Isaac remained standing. He turned his glass around in his fingers and looked uncomfortable. For a moment it looked like he might also sit down. But then he seemed to make up his mind that he had to speak and set his glass on the table. Reaching into his pocket he produced a small object and flicked it open. Jude's notebook! He coughed and glancing at Ellie, appeared to be reassured by a smile and nod, and began.

'It is with mixed feelings that we come to this last meal together tonight as a family. You are on the threshold of a whole new adventure, taking with you our dearest wishes. We respect your decision to go just as you respect ours to stay.'

'Each of us is choosing to fulfil our respective duties to ourselves, to our families, friends and neighbours in unique ways. That is our right and our responsibility as individuals but also as citizens of this Community. We have responded differently to the situation before us but each choice is governed by a shared desire for the greater good. So, I too would like to propose the same toast, because it seems to fit. To us all.'

Once again everyone got to their feet, but as they raised their glasses they heard the sound of knocking at the front door of the cottage.

'Who's that I wonder?' said Nick to Eva who looked just as surprised as he did. He went to the door.

Everyone turned. At first it was difficult in the flickering candlelight but then as the door was opened and a figure stepped through they all recognised Mr Shampali. With him were his wife and their elderly parents. He stopped short when he saw the table and hung his head. The rest of his family huddled behind him. Nick was the first to recover.

'Mr Shampali. What a surprise. Do come in. How can we help you? We are just finishing dinner as you can see. Would you care to join us for a drink? You would be most welcome.'

Pete stood and offered his chair as did Hannah and Hope. Jude seemed caught off guard but his mother nudged him and he too stood up. All of the visitors hesitated but, reassured by Nick's tone eased themselves into chairs and rested their hands on the table, all the time watching Mr Shampali. It was clear he was to be their spokesperson.

'I beg your pardon for interrupting you,' he murmured. 'It is an imposition.'

Nick was about to protest when Isaac cut in. His voice was ice cold.

'What is it that you want Shampali? I'm sure you can see this is a family occasion.'

Ellie gasped. Mr Shampali kept his eyes turned to the ground.

'I beg forgiveness. But I wished to have a word, if I may, with Mr Grigori.'

'Of course,' said Nick. 'What is it that you want to say?'

Mr Shampali took a deep breath.

'Mr Grigori, sir. My family and I are strangers here. We have no history with your Community and brought nothing but ourselves and what we could carry with us on our long journey to this place. We are not ignorant of the feelings that many here have towards us. But, like you, we wish to have a home where we feel we belong. We know' and he nodded towards Isaac, 'that can never be here on this island. So,' he paused 'we would ask if we could join you and your family tomorrow and sail to a new beginning and what we trust could be a better future.'

Hope looked across to Isaac expecting him to be delighted at the prospect of seeing the last of these people he so clearly despised. Instead he was standing with his hands clenched. If looks could kill, Shampali would have perished on the spot.

******   ******   ******

'You can't take those people with you!'

Isaac was quivering with rage. The door had hardly closed behind the Shampalis when he spat the words into Nick's face. Hope was sure they must have heard and ran to bolt the door and draw the curtains. Turning to the open fire, Nick lifted the poker and started to riddle air furiously into the embers before throwing on a couple of extra logs. The room had suddenly chilled.

Turning to face Isaac he crashed the poker onto the stone hearth. The whole room jumped. They looked like two pugilists squaring up for a bare knuckle fight. This was not going to be pretty.

'Isaac, this isn't up to you. You've made your decision, I'll make mine.'

Isaac pointed at Eva.

'She's my sister, you bastard. It's bad enough that you're taking her away from the one place where she has any chance of being safe. The idea that you'd risk her life even more by taking that bunch of wasters with you is insane. They've done nothing but drain us of resources since they got here. What makes you think they'll do any better somewhere else?'

'Shut up Isaac. You're not my keeper,' Eva was struggling to keep her voice steady. 'I'll make my own decisions. You've no right to try and tell us what we should or shouldn't do.'

Isaac slammed his hand on the table and made everything on it jump.

'I've every right! I'm your brother for God's sake. I've got a duty to you, and Hope. You're my flesh and blood. The Shampalis are nothing to me. They'll suck you dry, drain your energies, consume whatever you give them and you'll get nothing back. The parents are old and Shampali and his wife are wrecked. Life has beaten any energy they might have had out of them. They've had their turn. They're not our responsibility.'

'I think you'd better go Isaac, before any of us says something we're going to regret. If the Shampalis want to come with us then they can. It's not up to you to decide for them, or us.'

Hope was rooted to the spot and seemed incapable of dragging her eyes away from Isaac. What was he going to do next?

It was Ellie who unfroze the tableau. Crossing to Nick she wrapped her arms tightly round her brother. When they parted both were in tears as he stroked the hair off her forehead and kissed it. Then she moved to Eva who, sobbing, flung her arms around her. Finally she went to Hope, pulled her head to her shoulder and whispered in her ear.

'I'll always be with you Hope. Never forget that.'

Then she turned and, pushing past Isaac, unbolted the door and half fell, half stumbled into the darkness.

Jude was the first to react. Stepping out from the shadows and without a backward glance he ran after his mother.

Isaac went to the opening and shouted into the night.

'Ellie, Jude, where are you going? Come back.'

The only sound was the sea washing the shore. Isaac turned to look over his shoulder before he too went to follow them out into the darkness. As he prepared to slam the door behind him he hissed into the room.

'If anything happens to my sister I'll never forgive you as long as I live Nick Grigori. I swear.'

June 25th 2061

Although it was the shortest night of the year it felt like the longest. None of them could sleep so they spent the hours till dawn talking in low whispers, napping on chairs and sofas, checking through cupboards for any last minute additions to the bundles waiting to be loaded onto the small boats in the morning.

'I don't want to imagine what the atmosphere's like at Ellie and Isaac's,' Pete said to Hope.

Around three in the morning Hope threw off the blanket he had wrapped over them both and tiptoed downstairs. Her father's jumper lay where he'd dropped it on the sofa and she slipped it over her head. The sleeves fell across her hands and it reached almost to her knees. Folding back the cuffs, she pulled her boots on to bare feet and left by the front door.

Streaks of pale silver were beginning to appear on the horizon. Silhouettes of trees and cottages became moment by moment more distinct, hedging the view as the sun rose. She skirted a tangle of old bushes.

The tide was very low. Drifting around the headland, Hope was surprised to see a figure perched on the rocks revealed by the receding waters and stretching out like rugged fingers into the sea.

She hesitated. The last person she wanted to talk to was Isaac and from a distance it looked like him. But as the man stood up and turned to pick his way back over the slippery surfaces she realised with a start that it was Jude.

Hope had hardly spoken to her cousin in weeks and felt a familiar pang of guilt. They had been close as children and now she had little sense of how he was feeling. When had they drifted so far apart?

Jude glanced up. For a moment he also seemed uncertain how to respond to her presence but then he continued striding towards the beach. They met at the point where sand became shingle and the air was sharp with the smell of salty seaweed.

Hope reached out but Jude stayed where he was, hands thrust into the pockets of his jeans. She ignored the signals but his body was wooden, giving nothing away.

'That was a horrible night,' she murmured.

Pulling away Jude set off along the shingle and she fell into step beside him.

'Is your father very angry?' she asked.

Jude nodded, running his hand through his hair.

'I don't know what to do. I've never seen him like this.'

It was the most open thing he'd said to her in months.

'How's your mum?'

He took a few deep gulps of breath before replying.

'She can't stop crying. I can't bear to see her so upset.'

Hope went to touch his arm but he shrugged her off again and strode away. She ran to keep up with him.

'Jude, it's OK. I want to help.'

'That's the trouble though isn't it? You can't help, nobody can. Your bloody father's on his crusade to save the world and nobody's going to stop him.'

'Don't talk like that Jude. It's not Dad's fault. He can't help the way he thinks. This is what he believes in. It's what I believe in.'

'Well that's alright for you. You can have your high minded principles and act like everyone else is selfish and evil. But look at the trouble it causes. Mum's falling apart, Dad's gone crazy and you, what have you done it for? A bunch of people that aren't even family, are always going to be trouble and'll never be able to pay you back.'

He marched off and she caught up with him as he reached the path that wound upwards into the dunes.

'It's not like that Jude. You make it sound like we don't care about anyone but ourselves and that's not true.'

'Of course you 'care', Hope. That's all people like you and your saintly father ever do. You 'care.' You go out of your way to 'care' for people, to be 'kind', to 'share.' But what difference does any of this 'caring' you're so proud of make? It might warm a few hearts for a while, make you feel better. But, in the long run, it solves nothing. It makes things worse. It stops you from taking the sorts of decisions that could make all the difference to this Community, or indeed any community, help us survive. Where's the fairness you and your lot are so fond of talking about in that?'

And without another word he left, running and stumbling up into the dunes till he disappeared from sight.

Hope watched him go and then turned and made her way slowly back to the cottage. She knew this was what failure felt like.

******   ******   ******

'Right, is that everything?'

Eva took one last look around the front room. It was stripped, all the everyday objects that had made it theirs either packed away or in the boat.

The two vessels were trimmed and ready. The four older Shampalis were already onboard theirs. Pete had helped to piggy back them one at a time through the waves. They sat like stones, bundled in coats and blankets. Their boat, low in the water, had seen better days, but the sea was calm and it was not to be a long journey.

Pete, Hannah and their parents Jim and Flora were in the second, larger boat with Abe and Sarai. Hope clambered in and helped Eva over the side. Nick was the last to board.

They pulled up anchors and fired up the motors, easing the crafts away from the shore. As far as they could see no one was watching them leave.

Hope hadn't known what to expect at their departure, but it wasn't this. They would be visible from many of the cottages dotted along the shoreline and the few nestled in the dunes.

'I wonder if anyone's watching behind the curtains?' she said to her father. 'I thought we meant something to people, that someone would at least come and say goodbye.'

Nick had his hand on the tiller, skilfully steering the boat along the edge of the shore, keeping a sharp look out for rocks.'

'Someone did,' he said. 'Isaac was waiting when I came down here to start loading this morning.'

A second surprise.

'What did he say?' asked Hope.

'Nothing much. He was below decks checking over the Shampali's boat, it's not the most seaworthy. But he said it was the least he could do after everything that had happened last night.'

Hope glanced back at the Shampali's boat. It was moving more slowly through the water than theirs but making headway.

'What was he like?'

'He seemed resigned to the situation, focused. Like he'd made peace with it.'

'Did he apologise for what he'd said last night?'

Nick shot her his 'you have to be kidding' look.

'Apologising is not one of your Uncle Isaac's defining characteristics.'

She faced forward and, feeling the breeze, closed her eyes to savour the moment. The tide was well out. Soon they would be exposed to the open sea.

Suddenly Pete shouted.

'Look, a boat!'

Sure enough, a tiny craft had slipped from a cove on the most easterly side of the island and was heading straight towards them.

Eva pulled binoculars from a bag at her feet and handed them to Nick. He trained them towards the boat as it gained on them.

'It's a woman. Hang on, it's difficult to see but I think, maybe, yes, it's Ellie!'

The Shampalis had also seen the boat, shut off their engine and were bobbing in the waves. It took just a few moments for Ellie to reach them. When she did, she flung over a rope and threw up a bag. Several pairs of hands stretched down and she was half lifted, half dragged up and over the side.

She ran to the prow and waved to Nick and the rest of the family. Cupping her hands over her mouth she shouted. It must have taken all her strength, but the words carried over the waves.

'I'm coming with you.'

Hope and Eva moved to the stern to join Nick and the three of them cheered and punched the air. It was all Nick could do to control his joy and hold the rudder. Eva was crying and laughing at the same time.

'What's happened? Why has she come?'

'I don't care why, we'll find out soon enough,' said Nick. 'Let's get going. I'm just glad she's here. It's probably a good idea to put as much distance between her and Isaac as we can.'

Both crews set to unfurling sails. They would hug the shoreline for a couple of hours and then head northwards to the estuary where their new home awaited.

Hope could see her aunt. She was standing at the prow of the boat, the wind tugging at her hair. Even from this distance she could sense that she was smiling.

As soon as they hit the open sea the wind caught their sails and they picked up speed. A distance opened up between the two boats but they maintained clear lines of sight between themselves. The sun was well up into the sky, the air warm and comforting on her skin. Hope could feel herself, for the first time for weeks, beginning to relax and look forward. Pete stared ahead.

After a few hours, Eva unpacked some sandwiches and handed them around. At first Hope shook her head but her mother insisted.

'We need to eat.'

Hope bit into the crust, savouring the tang of the chutneys they'd spread the night before and lay back, looking up into the clear blueness till the sun soaked into her face, drying the spray that was touching her lips with saltiness. She closed her eyes and breathed in the bright summer morning air. As she filled her lungs to bursting point with its promise Pete leaned over her and she opened her eyes and looked up at him.

'I never want this moment, this feeling, to end.'

And then it did.

******   ******   ******

They had no warning. They wouldn't have known a thing.

The explosion shattered the Shampali's boat into a million pieces that spread across the sky and rained down into the sea forming a blackened raft.

For an instant, no one moved. It was Nick who reacted quickest. He swung the tiller, started the process of tacking back to the wreckage through the wash it had created, bellowing as loudly as he could.

'Ellie!'

Pandemonium erupted. They became a screaming and howling body of sound from all directions on the deck. Everyone moved at once, tumbling from side to side as the boat was driven back through the waves.

'No, no, no,' wailed Hope and clung to her mother. Pete was hanging over the side, everyone was sobbing. The shock was so great that none of them could drag their eyes away from the carnage and they raked over it again and again pleading for some miracle.

They knew it was pointless. Nothing and no one could have survived. But the finality of the loss would not sink in and seemed to numb them. They tacked up and down for more than an hour through the mass of driftwood that was all that remained of everything that had once been the Shampalis, Ellie and the boat.

Barely a hundred metres from the shore they dropped anchor and furled the sails. Everywhere they looked was wreckage, mostly unrecognisable but occasionally something familiar would float into view. They had stepped, in an instant, from one world where life could be hard but had some certainties, to another where the only certainty was despair.

Hope sat in the prow, staring over the side. They never found Ellie's body. They did however find Shampali. He was floating, face down, draped over a jagged plank that bobbed about on the surface. They all watched him for a while until the wood washed against another plank and the jolt caused him to slip from his moorings. He sank beneath the surface and disappeared forever. Everyone bowed their heads. No one spoke.

******   ******   ******

Jude had overslept and woke to sunlight streaming through his bedroom window. For a moment he lay still, disorientated, and then remembering the night before, threw off the covers and tumbled downstairs.

The house was deserted. There were signs of someone having had an early breakfast but both of his parents' coats had gone. After last night's arguments they must have wanted to let him sleep.

He shivered. The bitterness of the fighting had been shocking. He'd never seen his mother so fired up.

'How can you say such things? Be so unfeeling towards another human being?' she'd screamed. 'They're flesh and blood; they've been to hell and back.'

Isaac had refused to listen.

'You know how I feel. I've made it clear what I think. I'm not going to change my mind.'

She'd flung herself at him and pummelled his body with her fists, beside herself with impotent fury. Jude shuddered trying to erase the memory, seeing his father raising his arm to Ellie and batter her away. Her head had smashed on the hard stone fireplace.

'Leave her alone,' he'd screamed. She was almost unconscious, blood streaming from her forehead. Gathering up her slender body he'd carried her to the sofa, laying her on the cushions and running to get water and cloths to staunch the flow. Isaac made towards her then stopped, turned on his heel and stormed out of the house. Jude had no idea when or if he'd come back.

It had taken some time to clean up the wound, and even longer to stop the tears. He felt helpless, trapped by the warring factions of his family.

'I'm so sorry Jude. You shouldn't have to deal with this,' Ellie whispered.

He had sat with his mother's head on his lap for a while, appearing torn between duty and love, stroking her hair away from her face. When he was sure she was asleep he eased himself off the sofa and rested her head on cushions, wrapping a blanket over her thin body. She sighed and then nestled into the warmth of the space he'd vacated. He needed air.

Spotting Hope coming towards him at the shoreline he'd almost turned away. It was as if he couldn't face talking about what had happened, not wanting to expose his father to any further criticism. He would know that if Hope heard what Isaac had done there would be no way of protecting him. Isaac had lost control, broken a taboo. Nick would ride in to save his sister and family loyalties would come crashing down around them all. They had opened a Pandora's Box of hatred with the potential to shatter all of their relationships into a million unfixable piercing shards.

Jude walked up and down on the beach for almost an hour after leaving Hope, eventually tiptoeing past his mother's sleeping form and falling, exhausted, into his bed just before dawn.

When he woke the house was empty.

He'd not seen the note at first. It was tucked under the book that Isaac was reading, and dropped to the floor as he'd lifted it to clear the table. A single sheet with his father's name printed on one side. He recognised his mother's handwriting.

'I can't do this any longer. I'm leaving with Nick.'

It wasn't signed.

There had barely been time to think when he heard footsteps approaching, the door opened and Isaac entered. Without a word Jude handed his father the note. Isaac took a few seconds to absorb what it said and then the colour drained from his face. He looked like he would faint.

'When, how?' Isaac stared wildly at his son. 'Where is she?'

'I don't know. I left her sleeping here. When I came down she was gone. I've only just found the note.'

Isaac turned on his heels, ran out of the door and back along the path to the place where they moored their small dinghy, Jude following.

The dinghy was gone.

Isaac raced along the beach, heading for the spot where Nick and the Shampalis had, just hours before, set sail. Jude was close behind. His father ran up and down, shouting Ellie's name across the empty waves.

There was nothing.

Isaac threw himself to the ground, clawing at the shingle and beating his fists against it till they bled, oblivious to the waves that lapped around him, soaking him through.

'You've driven her away,' Jude screamed. 'She might never come back.'

Eventually he half lifted, half dragged his father from the water, staggering under his weight and dropped him on dry sand.

Isaac clambered to his feet and strode into the water.

'Ellie, come back. I'm sorry, I didn't mean it. Ellie, I need you.'

He was quickly out of his depth and flung himself into the waves. Every time he broke the surface he shouted, but the weight of his clothes started to pull him under. The currents were strong here.

Jude appeared to realise that his father was drifting dangerously far from the shore. Without hesitation he pulled off his shoes and clothes and ran into the waves, powering towards him. When he reached Isaac he turned him onto his back and looped his arm round his neck, making his way in parallel to the beach and towards some rocks where they would be able to scramble to safety. It took every ounce of his energy, but he managed it. They both lay panting. The sun was well up, but Isaac soon began to shiver.

'Dad, come on. You can't stay here. We need to get you to the house.'

They staggered up the shore and back to the cottage, Isaac half dazed, stopping every few steps to cough and splutter.

Jude manhandled Isaac through the door. It looked like he might crumple to the ground. Pulling a jumper over himself Jude began to strip his father's soaking clothes, using the blanket that he'd wrapped around his mother to rub him briskly dry.

'You're in shock, you need to get warm, Dad. Here...' Jude threw another blanket across his shoulders and ran upstairs to get dry clothes. Grabbing trousers for himself en route he hurried back down. Isaac hadn't moved.

Jude set about pulling clothes over his father's head and legs. He knelt at his feet when he'd finished and looked long and hard into his father's eyes. They were empty, vacant, the skin around them pallid. Jude didn't like what he saw.

'I'll get you something hot to drink, Dad. Stay there, try and warm up.'

His back was turned and he sensed rather than heard movement. Glancing over his shoulder he was astonished to see his father walking towards the door.

'No, Dad, you can't go out. You need to rest. You've had a shock.'

Appearing to notice his son for the first time, Isaac stopped in his tracks, a look of anguish on his face.

Jude made tea wrapping his father's hands round the mug and helping him to sip. The colour was starting to return to Isaac's cheeks, but he still appeared dazed. His eyes fell on the note he'd dropped and he picked it up. It trembled in his hand and before Jude could stop him he'd let the mug slip from his fingers and hugged the note to his chest. Falling forward onto his knees he gave a huge moaning sigh that shook his body. Jude wondered if he was ever going to breathe again.

And then the tears came.

Jude had never seen his father cry, let alone give himself up to such soulful sadness as he did that day. He tried to comfort him but it was futile. The man was hunched over, rocking, inconsolable, a picture of remorse and desolation.

'Ellie, Ellie. What have I done? What have I done?'

Jude lost track of time. He couldn't quite believe his mother had finally defied Isaac and really gone.

'Dad, we'll find a way to contact her. Once they're settled, Nick and Hope will get a message to us.'

Isaac moaned.

'Maybe you should try to go to sleep for a bit Dad. There's nothing we can do today. I can try and contact them in a few days. I might not be able to for a while but at least I can try. It's not like she's dead. There's always a chance. She might come back.'

He'd hoped these would be words of comfort, but instead Isaac's grief appeared to intensify. He grabbed Jude's wrists and shook him hard.

'This is my fault. If anything's happened to your mother...' his voice trailed off. Jude extricated himself from his father's grip and put an arm awkwardly round his shoulders.

'She'll be fine Dad. She's just gone away with Uncle Nick and the others. They'll look after her, don't worry.'

He paused. There was more that needed to be said but he was not sure if it was his place to say it. But there was no one else. He had a duty to fulfil.

'I'll miss her too you know, Dad. All she ever did was to love you, try to do the right thing by both of us. But you hurt her, you made her scared. You can't blame her for running away, you drove her to it. I don't hate you Dad, but I can't ever forgive you. Everything that's happened, it's down to you.'

****** ****** ******

There was nothing more they could do. They turned the remaining boat northwards and carried on.

The wind was behind them and they made good speed, hugging the coastline, going through the motions of trimming sails and catching the breeze, each lost in grief.

Nick had the rudder and Eva sat beside him. They exchanged only a few words and every so often she would reach up and squeeze his hand. She could see that Pete was watching Hope, Flora and Jim had Hannah between them.

'We're close enough to shore to land and camp for the night,' said Nick to Jim. 'Should we risk it do you think?'

Jim nodded. 'We can take turns to stand guard and it might be good to get a fire going and have a proper meal. There are plenty of coves and inlets we can slip into.'

They camped in dunes that ran down to the shore. Pete, Hannah and Hope hunted round for driftwood and walked along to a small coppice of trees for extra kindling. By nightfall they had eaten the food they'd brought with them and were gathered round the embers, each of them turning over the events of the day, trying to piece together what might have happened.

'I don't understand why it exploded,' said Flora. 'I know it was an old boat, but...'

Jim shrugged his shoulders 'They were pushing to keep up. It could have caused a problem.'

Pete shook his head. 'I wouldn't have thought so, Dad. Something has to have gone seriously wrong. Something technical.'

Nobody spoke. It was Hope who finally said what they were all thinking.

'Was it, could it have been deliberate?'

Nick reached out and drew her to him. As she sobbed into his chest he looked over her heaving shoulders at Eva and raised his eyebrows.

She bit her lip. It was too horrible to contemplate.

******   ******   ******

The next day they continued on their journey, weaving along the coastline and keeping land always in their sights. Eventually they reached a wide estuary and turned west, sailing towards the sunset.

'There it is,' called Jim.

In the distance they could see clusters of houses nestled round a cove and make out people moving between them, smoke rising from fires. A group of children spotted their boat and ran down to the water's edge to greet them. Row upon row of multi coloured pieces of fabric, fluttering in the evening sunlight, hung from ropes strung between trees, rocks, bushes and poles, dancing in the wind, marking the entrance to the settlement. The sound of bells and wind chimes called to them over the waves.

Hope stood anchored to her father at the prow of the boat. In spite of everything, the unanswered questions, grief and sadness, she felt a sense of peace.

'This is our chance to start again, Dad.'

Nick hugged her tight. They would be strong together. They had to be.

That night the skies were alight with dancing colours. They had become accustomed to the increasing numbers of aurora borealis displays over the years, but on this occasion the curtains of light that swept above them held an intensity Hope had never known before.

'Something good's going to happen here, it has to,' she breathed. 'But we have to believe.'

July 21st 2061

Jude woke early each morning, made his way to the crypt, turned on the computer, tried to reach Nick and get a message to his mother. Each day he'd looked for a response. Nothing.

'It's to be expected, Dad. They'll take time to settle, build trust, and make certain that it's safe. They'll want to reassure themselves that there are firewalls at least as secure as ours are before opening up any channels of communication. We've got to be patient.'

But it was hard for Jude. He missed them more than he had imagined. He needed his mother for comfort and compassion. And even though they'd spent so little time together, he missed Hope. He found himself remembering happier times when they'd seemed carefree and life had been so much simpler. It had all passed in a flash. Time was such a trickster.

Isaac's behaviour caused Jude more and more concern each day.

'Dad, you have to eat, you're going to make yourself ill,' he'd said one evening as he gathered up one of many picked over meals that he'd made to try to tempt him.

'I'm not hungry,' shrugged his father. 'Lost my appetite.'

It was not yesterday's excuse when, fretful and irritated he'd swept the plate to the floor, screaming:

'This is nothing like your mother would have made.'

He had apologised and Jude, adopting the approach of passive resistance he'd seen Ellie use for so many years, said nothing. But inside he had started to hate Isaac.

'Any word about your mother?' Andrew asked as they walked through the houses on their way to check on some of the outlying farms. 'How long's it been now?'

Andrew was a year or so younger than Jude. He had been part of the original group that had travelled up from the village and joined the island Community years previously when Naomi was still alive.

'Nothing,' Jude muttered and changed the subject. He didn't find talking about his mother's absence helped, just made it feel more real.

Isaac was full of self pity.

'They'll be glad Ellie's left me,' he had moaned one night. 'I've always known they don't approve. Sarai actively dislikes me. She never thought I was good enough for her daughter.'

Jude had sometimes suspected as much, but was not going to make his father feel even worse by agreeing with him. He had always felt divided loyalties when it came to the relationship between his grandparents and Isaac. Some months previously, Jude had been on his way out one morning when he had turned the corner of the church and come across his grandmother, leaning on a gravestone. He had guessed she was waiting for him and felt ambushed.

'Jude!' she said.

'Good morning Gran.'

He had tried to walk by but Sarai stood up, blocking his path.

'I've been hoping to catch you for a while now. Have you got a minute?'

'I'm sorry Gran, this isn't a good time.'

She had remained where she was and he was forced to stop or push past her. Sarai had fallen into step beside him, placing one hand on his arm to slow him to her pace.

'Have you had breakfast yet?'

He shrugged.

'Not really.'

'Not really. What sort of answer's that? Come along with me and I'll make you some. Your grandad will be so happy to catch up with you.'

He could see that she wasn't going to be dissuaded and had allowed himself to be steered to their cottage. It was a tiny place, one of a row of six single storey buildings each with gates and gardens and paths leading to wooden front doors that opened into living rooms. His grandparents' door was cornflower blue.

'The colour of the eyes of her indoors' Abe had said with a twinkle when he'd helped him with the painting.

'Abe, look who's here,' Sarai had called as they went in.

His grandfather looked up from the boots he was polishing.

'Well, well if it isn't young Jude,' he said with a warm smile. 'You'll be wanting breakfast I expect?'

He was sure they had planned this but it was impossible not to relax in their company. Sarai had made herself busy in the tiny kitchen while Abe carried on with his boots, asking Jude about how he'd been and showing real interest in everything he said.

When Sarai brought through eggs and porridge he had sniffed appreciatively.

'Lovely, lass. Come on Jude, get sat down. Don't want this to go cold.'

He dragged a chair to the table and tucked in as directed. When he'd finished Sarai gathered up their plates.

'Thanks Gran.'

He had sensed they weren't finished with him and braced himself for what was to come. It was Abe who had taken the lead.

'So, young man, how's your dad and your mum these days?'

'We're doing OK thanks. Keeping busy.'

'Can't be easy for you though Jude, your dad having so much responsibility and him turning to you for help all the time.'

Sarai had reached across the table and cupped one of Jude's hands in hers, curling her fingers around it. Her skin was warm and smooth.

'You can only do your best love. You're a good lad.'

No one had spoken for a few moments. Jude fought hard to stay calm, determined not to reveal how worried he had been becoming about his parents or to be the first to break the silence. In the end, it was Abe who had spoken next.

'We know you want to be loyal Jude and that does you credit. They're your parents after all. Isaac's your father, it's right you show respect towards him. But Jude, your grandma and I have known your mother's not been herself for a long time. She doesn't say anything, but we can tell things aren't right. We're her parents after all, and you get to know your own child. You're not going to be giving away any secrets here.'

'Does she say anything to you?' asked Sarai.

Jude had realised too late that he should never have allowed himself to be drawn into this conversation. He pushed his chair back from the table and stood.

'Sorry Gran, I don't know anything.'

'Do your mum and dad have words at times Jude? Like the other night after the meeting your father called at the Gathering House?' asked Abe. 'It's alright to tell us, Jude. I can't imagine after what was said that she wouldn't have spoken up when you all got home. Do they argue the pair of them?'

It had been no good trying to cover up, they were too persistent, too intuitive.

He nodded.

'Right, guessed as much. And I'm thinking things sometimes get a bit heated do they? What with your dad's strong opinions and your mum not exactly seeing eye to eye with him.'

Jude nodded again.

'How bad does it get, Jude?'

'I don't know...they argue...sometimes we're all upset...'

Abe had thumped his fist on the table making the crockery, Jude and Sarai jump.

'God help me, if he so much as lays a finger on her, I'll kill him.'

Sarai looked horrified.

'Come on Jude, you've got to tell us.'

Bit by bit they had dragged the story out of him. Not just what they'd said to each other after events like the Gathering House meeting when it had become obvious that Isaac and Nick were to go their separate ways, but everything else he'd been forced to live with for so long. The sneering and sarcasm Isaac heaped on Nick every time his name was mentioned; the despising of incomers, particularly those like the Shampalis whose heritage was so very different from their own. And, most of all, the fear of what might become of them all if they failed to head off the growing pressure on resources for the many if they continued to over protect the few.

'It's not fair,' he'd muttered.

'What's not fair, son?'

'Dad's only ever tried to do the right thing but none of you will listen. You push him out; make him feel like he's doing something he shouldn't, like he doesn't care. And now Mum's upset and Dad doesn't talk to her and I don't know what to do.'

Jude's grandparents had looked horrified. They disliked Isaac, it was true, felt protective of Ellie. Concern for her welfare had been more important to them than anything.

'Jude, listen,' said Abe. 'I'm sorry about earlier. But it's natural, son. Mums and dads, we worry about our kids, try to protect them. Sometimes we get a bit carried away.'

Sarai had put her arms around Jude.

'You know, you can always talk to us, call in whenever you can. Your mum and dad can too if they ever want to.'

Jude nodded.

'I know, thanks. I'm glad you're here.'

Abe had walked him down the path.

'Should I come back with you now, Jude? Maybe talk to your dad?'

He'd hesitated. It was very tempting.

'Maybe leave it for now, Granddad. I'm not sure how Dad'd take to a visit and he'll be wondering where I've been all this time. He'll be working. I'll tell him you want to see him though.'

Looking back now Jude recognised that it had been good to off load to his grandparents. Now they'd left with Nick he missed them not being on the island. He'd been able to say things to them he'd never have said to either of his parents. Perhaps he should have spoken to them sooner, they'd been more understanding than he could have hoped and they were family, after all.

Jude turned that conversation with his grandparents six months before over in his mind. Had he been disloyal? He didn't think so, but it was hard to know. He felt like he walked a tightrope between his mother and father. And he had long ago lost any certainty about what he could expect from them as parents.

He had to hope that once they'd managed to recontact each other things in the family as a whole would get better. Maybe you just had to accept sometimes that people couldn't live together. It didn't mean you couldn't still be a family.

Jude and Andrew finished their work on the farms and prepared to make their separate ways home.

'I hope you hear from your mum soon,' said Andrew. 'Try not to worry. The others'll take care of her.'

As he was passing the church Jude decided to try once more to see if there were any messages for him. It was empty, peaceful, a sanctuary after everything that had happened and somewhere he felt safe. Taking a huge metal key out of his pocket he crossed the aisle, weaving between ancient pews polished to a dark sheen by years of use and placed it in the lock of the door to the crypt where the Project's computer was kept. How he longed for news.

******   ******   ******

Jude stared at the screen. There was a message.

Dear Jude,

Forgive me, I have so little time. No words can make this anything other than it is.

Your mum has been killed.

The boat that she and the Shampalis were on exploded around three hours after we set sail from the island. There was no warning, nothing to suggest a problem. We searched and searched through wreckage, but we found no trace of her.

All any of us have been able to ask ever since is why?

Mum, Dad, Flora, Jim, Hannah, Grandpa and Grandma, Pete and I are safe.

The Shampalis thought they'd be safe with us and have all died.

We have the protection of a new home; they have been lost at sea in an instant.

I am so very sorry. Please tell your father. I would give anything to be with you now.

Your loving cousin, Hope.

He read the words over and over. Killed? His mother? In the tiny confines of the crypt he could hear his heart pounding. He grabbed the table, thinking for a moment he might faint.

He tried to focus. An explosion? Wreckage? No trace? And why had his mother been with the Shampalis and not the family?

There was a sudden creaking sound and the heavy door of the crypt swung open. It was Isaac.

'Jude, what have you been doing all this time? I've been waiting at home for you. How long have you had this portal open? You know it's dangerous to be online for more than a few minutes.'

Isaac squeezed round the table reaching over to the keyboard. Jude was transfixed, staring at the screen. His father, at first more interested in closing down the communication, instead read Hope's message.

Jude stumbled out of the room, Isaac following. They fell onto a pew, Jude hunched forward, inconsolable. Isaac made no attempt to comfort him. Eventually Jude sat up and wiped the back of his arm across his eyes.

'I can't believe this, Dad.'

His father was deathly white. Reaching across, Jude felt his hand. It was icy cold. Staring wildly, Isaac got to his feet.

'I have to go to her.'

He began to make his way down the aisle to the door, each step a visible effort. Staggering, he stopped and rested his body against the final pew, breathing hard. Jude paused, suddenly afraid.

'Are you alright, Dad?'

Isaac muttered something Jude couldn't catch and he leaned his face closer to his father's mouth. Isaac's body suddenly convulsed and he doubled over in pain, clutching his hands to his chest. Jude, caught off guard, couldn't support him and had to let him fall to the floor. Bubbles were forming like foam at his mouth.

Cradling his father's head in his hands, Jude grabbed a kneeler to rest it on. He pulled his jacket off and wrapped it over his father's quivering body.

He had no idea what to do, but he managed to turn Isaac on his side.

'Dad, stay with me, come on, what can I do, where does it hurt?'

His father was trying to speak, all the time clutching his hands to his chest. Jude leaned in closer.

'I'm sorry, son, I'm sorry. I didn't mean to hurt her.'

Assuming he was referring to the last fateful night that the three of them had been together Jude tried to comfort him.

'I know Dad, it's ok. It was an accident.'

Isaac's eyes seemed to clear for an instant and he tried to lift his head.

'She shouldn't have gone. She shouldn't have got in the boat. It wasn't meant for her.'

The voice was weak, but the words distinct. Jude, distracted momentarily, turned to look his father in the eyes.

'What do you mean? What wasn't meant for her?'

Isaac's eyes started to close. Jude shook him.

'What Dad? What are you talking about?'

Isaac's head lolled to the side. Jude looked down at the man he'd tried so hard to please all his life. The man he had feared and always felt he'd failed. The man who had driven away his mother.

As he stared at him Jude turned over everything that had happened.

Suddenly it all made sense.

Isaac's body appeared to shrivel up like shed skin and Jude dropped him where he lay, pushing back on his heels and crying for his mother.

Fate had cheated him of the one thing he could have done to avenge her.

Correspondence

August 2061

Hope, Your message got through. Jude

Dearest Jude,
 It was so good to hear from you. How are you? I think of you all the time. What is the news? We miss Ellie so much. I wish I could be with you. I will check every day for any message.
 Your loving cousin, Hope

Hope, I also have news. My father died last week. We buried him next to the church. I am alone. Jude

Dearest Jude,
 We are so shocked and saddened to hear this news. How did he die? Was it an accident? How are you managing? We all send our love to you. Hope

Hope, Thank you, but do not trouble yourselves with anxiety for me. He died suddenly, as if his heart burst when he learned that Mum had gone. I was with him. Life is very different now. Jude

Dearest Jude
 How terrible for you. You must miss them both so much. At least they are together now and at peace. I hate to think of you alone. Hope

Hope, If there is any justice in an afterlife then I doubt they are together. They led very different lives.

Dearest Jude,

What do you mean? Hope

Hope, It's not a secret; we all know how unhappy they were together. Jude

Yes, but Jude, they were still your parents, they loved you.

That's an interesting perspective, Hope. It depends what you think love is.

Acceptance? Forgiveness?

Maybe, but there's some things people do that can't be forgiven.

Has something happened Jude?

Yes, I think so.

Is it to do with your mum?

Why do you ask?

It's just something Dad said to me the other day.

What did he say?

He can't understand how the boat exploded.

I might have an answer to that.

What do you think happened?

I don't think it was an accident.

What, the explosion?

It was sabotage. He never expected Mum to be on the boat.

Who?

My father.

Twenty Two Years Later

The Bay by a Lighthouse
September 17th 2083

Anna shivered. Her mother would have said someone had walked over her grave.

She pressed her face to the window, the circling beam of the lighthouse that stood alongside their cottage enabling her to see a little way into the night. Lashing rain and wind rattled the house to its bones. The sea was a rippling, living carpet sweeping from shoreline to horizon. Waves rolled forward like white tipped teeth, as they had done for millennia. Each wash sucked back over the shingle, before rolling forward again.

Where was Eli?

It was after midnight and the tide would be well on the turn, covering the causeway. He must have decided to stay on the mainland, but there was little shelter along the beach and nowhere offering beds for the night.

She shivered again. The room had chilled.

A whimper. Two babies sleeping. It was her turn to watch. She touched the foreheads of each with the back of her hand. Her mother had always told her she wouldn't know a long night till she'd sat up with a sick child.

The fire was still glowing and she would have liked to have thrown on another log. Instead, she wrapped herself in a faded checked blanket and stretched out on the sofa, allowing her eyes to focus on the embers and concentrating on slowing her breathing. It helped, but her mind was still alert to any sound or movement.

This was home, but she didn't feel sheltered.

Jerking awake from a light sleep, for a moment she didn't know where she was. Her sister was peering into the cradles and then moved to warm herself at the fire. Anna sat up.

'You OK, Erin?'

'Couldn't sleep. Where's Eli?'

'No sign. Must have missed the tide and had to stay.'

There was a pause.

'I'm worried,' whispered Anna.

'He'll be fine. He can take care of himself.'

Anna nodded. 'Hope so.'

The sisters sat in silence, the wind and rain continuing to give a running commentary on the state of the night.

'Do you want to go to bed? I don't mind taking over.'

Anna stretched back out on the sofa, pulling the blanket up to her shoulders.

'No, it's daft us both losing sleep. You go back to Callum.'

'OK, if you're sure.'

Anna snuggled back down. 'I'm sure.'

Tiptoeing back to the stairs Erin stopped halfway up and peered down into the cradles of the sleeping babies. At least they were safe.

She slid back into bed, folding herself round her husband. He stirred and turning pulled her close, stroking her hair and planting a kiss on her head.

'Eli's not come home.'

She sensed Callum tense. He pulled back and their eyes met.

'Not home?'

'And there's a storm brewing.'

'Yeah, I can hear.'

'Didn't want to say anything to Anna.'

'Course.'

They were whispering, their faces together.

'Did he say he'd be back tonight?'

'Yeah, but you know what he's like, Erin, he could've just missed the tide.'

'He knows to be careful.'

They lay for a moment listening to the wind whipping in from the sea.

'There's nothing we can do till it's light.'

'Will you go for him?'

'Yeah, I'll get the boat and head over.'

'I'm coming with you.'

'OK. Now get some sleep and try not to worry.'

They both knew that was impossible.

****** ****** ******

In Erin's nightmare she was trying to escape but the ground was quicksand. The sea was like a child having a tantrum, kicking and screaming, flinging itself onto the shingle, following up with a throaty sigh as it sank back into the depths. She was straining every muscle, pulling herself along hand over hand, legs useless.

She awoke in a cold sweat. A baby was wailing.

Tumbling out of bed, she stumbled downstairs and gathered up the bawling infant, willing her back to sleep.

The fire was out and the room was grown cold. After what seemed an age of rocking the baby's breathing slowed and she lowered her back into the cradle as she snuffled back into unconsciousness. The other child hadn't stirred. Erin smiled. Thank goodness Seb was a sound sleeper. They'd never have coped if both children had been like Lucy.

It was then that she noticed something was different. The whole house was silent. The wind and rain had stopped. And two coats were gone.

******   ******   ******

It was only a short distance from the lighthouse to the shore. The moment the wind had abated Callum had crept downstairs to find Anna lying awake. They had no real plan, just to get in the boat, find Eli and bring him home. They needed him.

It took half an hour to reach the mainland. They beached the boat, pulling it away from the tide line. Turning to make their way along the sand, they expected to have to search hard.

Eli lay where he had fallen, soaked through by the rain. His blood glistened in the moonlight, a dark stain on his chest, thick and sticky oozing into the sand and shingle.

They stumbled on him almost immediately, and both dropped to their knees. Anna turned him over, pulling his body towards her till she saw the knife.

'No, no, Eli! No!' She touched his face, cradling his head in her arms, calling his name and pushing his soaking hair from his eyes. 'What's happened, Eli, my darling? Say something, please, it's me. Anna.'

Callum wretched and without warning his stomach turned its contents out onto the sand. He wept for his friend. They had known there was danger, but not this. He clung to Anna and they sobbed.

It was a while before either of them could speak. Looking out to sea Callum picked out the first signs of dawn. He strained to hear if there was any sound, any watchers that might threaten them too.

'Anna, we have to go.'

His sister-in-law raised her head, her eyes dark, wet hollows. 'We're not leaving him.' Before he could stop her she had reached down, grasped the handle of the blade and in one movement heaved backwards, wrenching the knife from his stomach and flinging it as far as she could into the sea. Her body shook with the effort and she fell onto Eli's chest once again, wracked with grief.

When she had cried herself out, they lifted him. Using every ounce of their strength they managed to carry Eli's body to the boat and lowered it in. They pulled on the oars heading towards the lighthouse in a daze.

The boat's prow eventually crunched onto the shingle and from the cottage came the sound of a child crying. It was Seb. Anna didn't move. Callum reached out his arms to her, willing himself to be strong.

September 18th 2083

There'd been no time to think. They had simply grabbed anything they could and tumbled it into the little yacht, lifted the children from their cots and fled.

Callum sat at the rear holding the tiller as they tacked away and headed northwards, hugging the coastline. He hoped they were far enough out not to be seen, but he knew there were no guarantees. The sky was awash with dawn: orange, pinks and blues. The sea held them, caressing the boat's sides, shimmering like mercury in every direction.

Anna and Erin, each with a baby bundled up in as many clothes and blankets as they could find, sat opposite each other on either side of the central mast. Eli's body lay at their feet, covered in a rug, his head cradled on a pillow. He could have been sleeping.

The tide was on the turn and they were swept away from the land. When they were far enough out Callum raised the sail and the wind caught and urged them from the lighthouse, northwards along the coast.

They sliced through the water, a light spray blowing every so often into their faces. After the night's storms this was a perfect morning.

They saw the spire of a church in the distance, pointing into a cornflower sky. It stood at the edge of a headland that nestled round a crescent curved bay. Sloping sand stretched all the way to the water's edge. Callum steered as close to the shore as he dared and dropped anchor. He stripped off his outer layer of clothing, and half swam, half waded his way the short distance to land. He ran across the sand, clambered up a short flight of steps and reached a row of pebble dashed cottages. A man and woman stepped out and Callum fell into the waiting arms of his father and mother in law, words and explanations pouring from his lips.

Between them they used the power of the waves to lift the boat onto an ancient contraption of ropes and wheels. Sheer determination got it up the slope and away from the water. The woman from the cottage disappeared inside with the babies whilst the others formed a chain and emptied it of its provisions.

The cottage was the place where Erin and Anna had shared so many childhood memories with their parents. Once there had been neighbours and friends living close by, a whole community. But over time they had died or moved away so that now just Erin and Anna's parents, Stephen and Kirsty, remained.

The cottage drew them back into its comforting arms. Everyone fell into old roles. Erin big sistered and took care of both babies. Kirsty mothered and rocked her youngest daughter till Anna had wept herself to sleep. In the early evening Callum and his father-in-law, Stephen, collected shovels and went outside. When they returned it was almost dark.

Stephen crossed to Anna and knelt beside her. He smoothed the hair from his daughter's face, with hands covered in a dusting of fine dirt and touched her brow with his lips.

'We're ready Anna. Will you come?'

Wrapping a blanket round her shoulders, they eased her to her feet. Braced by her father and Callum, Anna made her way with the others to the church on the headland. Kirsty and Erin carried the children.

The grave was tucked under the wall, out of the wind, in full view of the sea. In the far distance they could see ancient statues: a man and a woman. They gazed out across the waves to the horizon as if keeping watch.

Her father's words at the graveside, Anna's tears, the waves on the shore, nothing broke through Erin's wall of silence. She kept her eyes on the statues bathed in the last rays of the evening light and only dragged them away when Lucy stirred in her arms and whimpered in her dreaming.

Eli, who had cast his protective shadow over them all for as long as she could remember, had gone, his body been laid to rest and they must sail on without him. She supposed that in time his tale would achieve the patina of so many other myths and legends and had no idea what the next chapter would hold. But although her heart continued to beat, Erin knew nothing would ever be the same.

****** ****** ******

Anna slept with her mother that night, cradled in her arms. On instinct, Callum and Erin took Lucy and Seb into their bed. To hold and be held, that was all that seemed to matter.

Callum couldn't sleep and pulled a chair to the window, half opening the curtain so he could see. He knew he wouldn't sleep and he wanted to play the patriarch, the man of the house that could, somehow, make everything better.

His thoughts turned to Eli, remembering the time Anna had first brought him home and introduced him to the family. She was besotted. He'd never seen such a change in a person. Eli had transformed her

She'd been perched on a stool in their kitchen, taking a break from helping her sister sort through cupboards and check they had enough food. Some time before, as supply chains for essentials were becoming more irregular every household had received a suggested list of basics to keep topped up in an attempt to prevent panic buying whenever a rumour of an impending shortage spread.

'Right reason, wrong thing to do,' Anna commented. 'All this is doing is raising anxiety, forcing up prices.'

She was right. Quite often the rumours proved ill founded. Not always of course, there'd been the odd time when shop shelves had emptied of certain products, but generally speaking they'd restocked within a matter of days, as long as people were patient.

Erin however had saved their list and pinned it to the cupboard door, just in case.

'So, tell us about this new man then, Anna,' Callum had teased. 'He's got to have made an impression if you're bringing him round!'

Anna blushed.

'I know. It's not like me is it? You be nice to him mind. And no acting weird. He still thinks my family's normal, whatever that means these days.'

The arrangement was that Eli would join them for supper. Callum had known, immediately, that this was a man in whom he could have complete confidence. Tall, dark, well built, he carried himself with the easy grace of an athlete. A sense of strength emanated from every part of his body but at the same time there was stillness and grace about him. He had presence. World and national news reports were becoming increasingly problematic. Callum felt Eli would care for his sister-in-law and help her through the challenges that they all suspected lay ahead.

Callum had grown up in the same neighbourhood as Erin and Anna. His parents and theirs were friends. He and Erin shared a history. They understood the local culture and were part of it. Eli had escaped from his home area to seek a better future and had no natural connection to this place. He was a stranger.

'How do you think people round here will react to Eli?' he'd asked Erin.

'Well, he'll be a challenge, that's for sure. He's charming, he's clever and he's hot! Might make some of the lads in the village put in a bit more of an effort.'

'You don't think they might freeze him out?'

'I'd hope not.'

Callum wasn't so sure.

Anna had always been more of a risk taker than Erin. It was no surprise that she was the one that couldn't settle for the familiar, had to make new connections. Whereas Erin could over think any situation, Anna took life as it came, didn't worry too much about what people thought. She'd been out with most of Callum's mates over the years, local lads. Eli outshone them all.

'So how did you two meet then?' Erin had asked as she ladled the stew and dishes of vegetables were passed from one to another.

Anna was pouring water flavoured with mint into glasses. She caught Eli's eye and blushed.

'I was dishing out food at the shelter and he kept coming back for seconds.'

Eli laughed and put his hands on his stomach. 'Cost me my delicate waistline, but it was the only way I could think of to get to speak to her. Then I volunteered for kitchen duties'

'Our first date we peeled spuds and chopped onions. Very romantic.'

The evening was full of warm laughter and shared memories. Towards the end, Callum looked up to see Eli and Anna each with an elbow on the table curling their fingers round each other. His thumb gently stroked her skin and as she dipped her head towards him he dropped a kiss onto her hair. She lifted her chin and smiled up into his eyes. In the flickering candlelight time stood still and, for Callum, the moment was caught in his memory like a photograph.

He would return to it often: a drop of hope from the past to light their darkening present.

Seb and then Lucy were born within a matter of weeks of each other just over a year later. The whole family had wept tears of pure joy at the arrival and blessing of two healthy children. Many of their neighbours had not been so fortunate.

'It's unbearable taking her out,' Erin whispered as she nursed Lucy in bed one night. 'I'm walking past girls I've known since I was a child and they look at me with such longing and envy. It's like we're strangers suddenly.'

'You can understand it though,' Callum replied. 'It's the same with the lads. It's in their eyes. They're wondering what's wrong with them. Why should our family be lucky? And twice over?'

'Do you think it'll pass? asked Erin biting her lip as she looked down at the tiny sleeping infant in her arms. 'The children'll grow and everyone'll get to know them. These are our friends. They're hurting now but surely they're happy for us? Besides, you know what folk are like in these parts. We've always cared for our own.'

Our own.

In the darkness of his in-laws' cottage Callum shifted in his chair, remembering. That was when his fears for the future had started. Outsiders, any strangers who were different, were a challenge to life as it had always been. And with challenge came risk.

There could be no doubt that Eli was different. He stood out, that's why Anna had noticed him, been attracted. But he had no history with the community and that community was becoming every day more fearful for itself.

He'd been a fool; he should have seen it coming. Local people hadn't known Eli like the family did and that ignorance bred fear, fear bred hatred and hatred bred violence.

Jealousy would also have been in the mix. Anna was one of their own but she'd chosen from outside. The men in particular didn't like that, felt slighted, not willing to credit this newcomer for his obvious skills and talents or to acknowledge their own shortcomings. It wasn't natural for a local girl not to want to be with a local boy, so it must be unnatural. After all, why else would anyone look outside of their own community for a mate? It was wrong. Perhaps a spell had been cast? Perhaps it was sorcery?

Callum remembered how they had pulled together as a family, refusing to allow themselves to believe the evidence of suspicion that was all around them. They preferred to think better of those they had known all their lives. It was nothing that was said. It was a way of looking, of acting when Eli was around.

Erin noticed it first and asked Callum about it.

'It's difficult to put a finger on anything specific. But I just get a feeling that people are wary of Eli,' she mused.

'Give it time. They just need to get to know him. Things are difficult, the stories and rumours are rife about what's happening up and down the country, tensions at the borders are getting worse and they're not used to strangers.'

Eli had joined Callum when he'd gone fishing with the other young men, but after a couple of trips had made his excuses. He didn't say why, but Callum could sense resentment at his easy mastery of a skill that in these parts men thought belonged to them. If Eli did fish, he did it alone. But the fear and resentment, instead of diminishing with time, seemed to burn its way deeper, fanned by ignorance and old loyalties.

Then, when there were choices to be made it started to feel as if they were being excluded.

One day, when milk was scarce Callum found himself reaching for the last carton in the local shop, sighing with relief that the children would not go without, only to have it snatched away by the shop keeper.

'I'm keeping that for a customer.'

'Come on Simon, it's not for me, it's for Seb and Lucy. They need milk.'

'Maybe you should have thought of that before bringing two more hungry mouths to feed into the world.'

He felt he'd been punched in the stomach and gasped. Simon Thompson. They'd been mates for years, grown up together and shared their first cigarettes. He walked home in a state of shock.

In the end, he began to feel that with some of his neighbours there was no such thing as community. Only 'your own.' And that proved a slippery category to define, changing almost daily in response to the amount of food, water, shelter and space they had.

Evidence of little acts of self protection, decisions about where individuals stood in the pecking order of entitlements, happened every day. It wasn't everyone, and on the surface nothing had changed.

'You don't quite know who you can trust anymore,' said Erin.

It was like the rules that they'd lived by all their lives were being rewritten.

'Some rules just aren't meant to be broken though are they?' said Callum.

The more time went on the more something he had never thought about started to dawn on him. This wasn't about neighbours and friends. This was about blood.

Blood was primeval. In families you shared genes, identity and heritage. You recognised yourself mirrored in another's being, understood their wants and needs, sympathised with them because 'they' were like 'you'. There was no challenge. You didn't have to accommodate or change.

It was easier that way.

Eli wasn't 'blood'. He should have been an asset, instead he was a threat. In his determination to be a good father and husband he had set a standard that some in the community could not hope to meet but he refused to settle for their mediocrity.

'He's not doing any harm,' said Anna. 'He just wants to be the best he can be. What's wrong with that?'

Nothing. But whoever had chosen to kill Eli had decided that he wasn't to live.

Pulling on his coat, Callum went outside and walked down to the beach. The moon and stars were out in a cloudless sky and he could see to the horizon in all directions. Everything was still and silent. Perhaps, after all, they had not been followed and the murderers were content to let them go.

Back at the cottage it was silent and he lay down on the settee, pulling a rug over himself, prepared to wait out the watch till dawn. But his eyes closed and, exhausted, he slept.

He jolted awake feeling instantly afraid though, for a moment, he couldn't remember why. Erin was kneeling by his side, her arms wrapped round him, her head on his chest. He lifted the rug; she crept under it and curled herself round him like a child. Her body trembled against his and he could feel her sobs. They lay together in mute grief.

In the morning the sun would still breathe life into the world, but Callum had no idea what to do next.

December 2084

Dearest Jude,

I have the best but also the saddest of news. My grandson has arrived safely into the world, but in giving him life our darling Rose Ellie finally gave up hers. She will never know the joy of mothering as I have. Pete and I are heartbroken. Hope

Dear Hope, It was with great sadness that I read of your loss. I know how precious your daughter was to you and Pete, please accept my condolences. I trust my great nephew brings you much joy and that he is healthy. Many would envy you his existence. Jude

He is perfect. My father would have adored him if he were still alive. I know he often longed for a son. We are calling him Jake.

I know people here who have similar longings, but to no avail.

I feel for them. Pete and I have lost our child, our most precious of gifts, but we have been luckier than so many others to have known the love all parents feel for their children.

Some parents, Hope, not all.

I'm sorry, Jude. You cannot share in my optimism I know, and I understand why.

Thank you. However, it is good to count blessings, even when they are few. Perhaps we are luckier than some.

I wish you would come and live with us, Jude. We are family after all and it's not good to be alone.

Hope, you know I have duties to fulfil for the Community here. They have chosen me to be their Chief Steward. I cannot let them down.

It is a heavy load you carry, dear cousin.

Many others have challenges that are harder I am sure. The world is not a pleasant place. I feel cocooned here, cut off from some of those realities, but we are still affected, as you are.

It's so unfair.

It is what it is, Hope

I wish there was more kindness between people.

The stories are of greater scarcities. People protect their own.

I know, and I fear for what that will mean for Jake.

Time will tell, Hope.

A Coastal Village
February 15th 2085

Thrusting the fork as deep as he could, Callum pressed down with his full weight and levered upwards, shaking out grass and weeds. Like most big tasks, the secret was not to rush but to nibble away, one mouthful at a time.

It had been almost two years. In the end they had decided to stay, but it hadn't proved an easy option. New responsibilities had brought changes in them all and Callum had needed tenacity.

Each night he crawled grey faced into bed, every muscle aching. He didn't know what he found more exhausting, the hard physical nature of their lives together or the constant thinking and planning that consumed them all. There was always a risk to identify and circumnavigate. So far they'd been left alone, protected by the isolated position of the cottage, but there were never any guarantees

He missed Eli.

He glanced up and saw Kirsty emerging from the cottage holding Seb and Lucy's hands. All three headed over to the henhouse, stopping every few steps for her to gather her breath. The children appeared unaware of her difficulties, chattering and tugging, eager to hunt for eggs. Kirsty took the steps into the shed one at a time and the door dropped to behind them.

Spurred on, Callum redoubled his efforts. His in-laws did their best, but they weren't getting any younger. This garden plot could be crucial.

By lunchtime he had cleared the ground ready for planting. Wheelbarrow loads of richly mulched soil had been turned into the earth and lines pegged out to mark where rows of newly planted vegetables would supplement produce already coming from raised beds and the fruit from their small orchard.

Stephen and Kirsty had long realised the value of self sufficiency as food supplies into the countryside became unpredictable and more and more people had moved out of the village heading north where the word was of safer living. They had stayed on; clinging to what was familiar and not wanting to move further from Erin and Anna.

In the two years since Eli's death, Callum had learned from his in-laws. He now knew how to keep roots from frosting, where to store fruit and vegetables over winter, which herbs would ease what pains and where to find them. He could read the weather from the sky, knew when hens would lay, how and where to set a trap. It was survival knowledge they were all determined to pass on to Lucy and Seb.

He and Anna and Erin were afraid for the children, their fears grown from tiny seeds and whispered exchanges, concerns expressed, pity and remorse germinating side by side. An illness in Stephen lasted weeks and needed constant nursing, a slowing of footsteps in Kirsty delayed a journey home, fatigue came on so suddenly and no amount of coaxing could dispel it. These behaviours triggered anxieties that put down roots. How could they manage?

'It's not fair. We're trapped,' Erin had wept, exhausted by nursing her mother and a succession of sleepless nights with Lucy. 'Mum's only going to get worse, more dependent. Dad's getting more and more forgetful. And I'm needed on the farm when I should be with Lucy. What are we going to do?'

March 2085

One night, unable to sleep, Callum tiptoed out of the house and down to the beach. There was no wind, the sky cloudless. He made his way to the church and Eli's grave. He needed to think.

The Milky Way felt close enough to touch. Great sweeping swirls of stars were unimaginable distances away and yet he could close one eye and block them out with his thumb. In eternity would any of this matter? He wanted to be a good parent, but all he could see ahead was heartbreak and all he had to offer was himself. It wasn't enough

Hearing footsteps he peered round the edge of the wall to see Stephen making his way towards him. He lowered himself onto the turf.

'Couldn't sleep,' he grunted.

'Me neither.'

In reality it was only moments, but it felt like a lifetime until Stephen broke the silence.

'We've been talking, me and Kirsty.'

'Talking?'

'Yes, about what we need to do.'

Callum shifted his body slightly but stayed staring up at the stars. 'Do about what?'

Stephen turned to his son-in-law and put his hands gently on each of his shoulders. There was a long pause.

'I think you know son.'

The dark graves huddled like conspirators around them as Stephen outlined the plan. Callum was struck by how little drama he attached to the proposals. When he'd finished they sat, listening to the gentle rhythm of waves breaking on the beach below them.

Stephen's face was silhouetted in the moonlight. His voice was steady.

'Kirsty and I, we're getting older. We all need to move.'

Callum swallowed hard. 'I don't know if I can leave here.'

Stephen placed his hand on Callum's. He felt its dry, papery warmth and fought to control his breathing.

'It's going to be hard, I'll give you that.' Stephen gave a deep sigh. 'I wish I could make it easier for you. But this is how it has to be. We have to do what's best for the children.

They sat till the first rays spread out across the horizon, silvering the separation between sky and sea with flickering flames of light.

'This hasn't changed,' said Stephen nodding at the view. 'It'll be here long after we're dead and buried. It's not like us, we're just mist. We have our time and then we vanish.'

They walked slowly back to the cottage. Before opening the door, Stephen turned to Callum.

'Kirsty and I will speak to Erin and Anna. They won't like it any more than you do, but we'll make them understand. At least we'll be together.'

He went inside. Callum went back down to the beach. As he looked out across the waves his fists clenched and unclenched, he realised his eyes were smarting and that he was having difficulty swallowing. If they moved on he would be leaving a place where he'd come to feel safe. If they joined a different community he'd have to put his trust again in people that weren't family. Callum shivered, pressing his hands to his stomach and turning his face to the stars, reaching for courage that he could only hope he had buried within him.

'No turning back,' he muttered.

August 2085

Dear Jude, I have given much thought to your proposals for managing the decisions you have to make about how you share resources on the island. A little for the many, or more for a few? Hope

Dear Hope, It is a question that has always been with us. It is simply that the focus is sharper when needs are greater than wants. Your father and mine disagreed on questions of rights, but not responsibilities. You and I are no different. Jude

Of course it's natural to protect your own. I would have taken a bullet for my daughter. Now I'd take a thousand more for her child.

And if he was very ill and could not survive without your care...?

I know it's difficult Jude. But what sort of people are we if we don't care for all of the vulnerable?

Pragmatists?

You will think me naive, Jude, but I want kindness in the world, and for everyone.

And do you trust kindness will come about naturally? Is that realistic? Is that what you see in the world?

Sometimes I do, yes.

And where there's not kindness, can we change anything?

We can learn from the past, of course we can.

And do we learn? Or wring our hands in despair when we should have acted sooner?

Everything's easier with hindsight.

But, Hope, none of this is a surprise. We should have seen all of it coming.

Meaning?

It's not enough to hope. I'm in charge here; people rely on me to make the tough choices. Someone has to.

October 1st 2085

The cottage had become little more than a shell.

The children thought of the promised new life as an adventure, a myth their parents and grandparents reinforced. Each day was filled with talk of opportunities that lay ahead, new friends to be made, fun to be had.

'Grandpa, will you miss us? Why can't you come too?' asked Lucy. 'Why?' had recently become her favourite question. She and Seb were playing at Stephen's feet. He was their rock, a steady presence to which they often clung.

Both children climbed onto the sofa and snuggled into their grandfather who, wrapping his arms round them, deposited a kiss on each mop of hair.

'I won't be far behind. Gran and I will be in the boat following you up the coast. Someone's got to bring that otherwise how am I going to do my fishing when we get there?'

'There'll be lots of other children in our new place,' Kirsty told them as she'd tucked them into bed on their last night in the cottage. 'Now, go to sleep. We've got a big day tomorrow.'

They snuggled down, tired but excited. Kirsty drew the curtains, a candle casting dancing shadows over the ceiling. She settled herself in a chair, not wanting to leave them. Seb hadn't changed since he was a baby. He fell asleep almost as soon as his head hit the pillow. Lucy looked ready to follow but she seemed to sense her grandmother's presence. She sat up; eyes hung about with sleep, her hair a ruffled golden crown.

'Grandma, I'm not tired'

Kirsty slipped under the covers. Lucy nestled into her, warm and trusting, snuffling and wriggling until she was comfortable. Her grandmother rocked and shushed her, their bodies connected through the rhythm of their respective heartbeats. In a few minutes Lucy's eyelids closed and her breathing deepened. She was asleep.

Downstairs the adults gathered round the fire, no one wanting to be the first to break the circle, preferring to extend the memory of this last night alone together. In the end it was Stephen who, heaving himself from his chair, hugged each of them and then he and Kirsty made their way through to their bedroom.

Callum, Erin and Anna remained. Eli's absence hung, unspoken, in the room.

Anna was half asleep, snuggled in a blanket. Erin wrapped her in big sister arms as she'd done when they were children and rocked her.

'Go to sleep,' she whispered. 'I'm here.'

October 2nd 2085

They were packed and ready. Callum would have charge of the larger wagon drawn by the two mares, laden with produce and difficult to steer. The children perched in the smaller cart. It was lighter and faster and Erin would take the reins with Anna beside her.

It looked as if the weather at least was going to be kind. Their plan was to use back roads and hug the shoreline as much as they could. With luck the carts should reach their destination before the tide turned for the night and be able to cross the causeway safely to the island before nightfall.

The boat meanwhile carried little more than the bare essentials for the journey up the coast, making it easier for Stephen and Kirsty to sail. All being well, they should make good time, but much depended on the wind and tides.

They had all known of the island to the north since childhood and had often referred to it as somewhere they might well find help. When times were less troubled Stephen and Kirsty had often visited with Erin and Anna. It had always had a reputation for peace and well being, a place where a community could thrive and indeed had done for thousands of years. None of the villagers who had already set out for it, or any of the refugees they had sometimes encountered making their way there had ever returned. Perhaps that was a good sign.

The children scampered around the yard while Callum, Stephen and Anna made last minute adjustments and checked the house and garden. Erin went to look for her mother and found her on the bed watching the family through the window.

'Love you, Mum.'

They sat together and held hands. Erin could feel her mother's skeletal frailty. She took up so large a place in her heart, but in reality her body had shrunk; though not her spirit. Kirsty reached inside her blouse, pulling out a silver chain and locket and hung it round Erin's neck.

'I want you to have this. My mother gave it to me before she died. Keep it always, do what it says, and one day, when the time comes, pass it to Lucy.'

Erin didn't need to look at the locket. It had been part of her life for as long as she could remember and bore a simple design, an oak tree, and two words: *Grow Strong*.

She helped her mother outside and down to the boat where Stephen was already waiting. Knowing they had to maintain an air of business as usual optimism as an artifice for the children, they had all exchanged hugs, shouting last minute instructions and farewells. Callum was to lead the convoy, steering his wagon with enormous skill out through the gates and onto the lane that eventually joined the road north. Erin and Anna followed, the children waving from the back of their cart to their grandparents who blew kisses from the gate.

As they passed the first corner, all their eyes turned forward. No one looked back. By lunchtime they had skirted round several villages, seeing no one but aware that each would contain people who had their reasons for staying, content to eke out an existence of sorts. These families kept their heads down, took their chances, asked nothing of others and gave nothing back.

Callum remained alert. His confidence and decisiveness had grown since his conversation with Stephen. He knew where they were going and what he had to do. But he still wished Eli was with them for he would have sensed danger. Callum only had his eyes and ears to warn him.

They rounded a corner and crested a gentle hill. The countryside stretched away in all directions, the sea a glittering carpet to their right. It was as good a place as any to stop. He pulled on the reins.

'We'll rest here for a while.'

Lucy and Seb clambered down and wandered over to the grassy verge. The two women unpacked fruit, bread and water and they settled together by the roadside to eat. Callum lay on the grass, allowing the warmth of the late summer sunshine to soak into his skin. He wondered if, in a different life, a family outing like this would have been normal.

After a while Erin and Anna collected up the remains of their meal, called to the children and helped them both back into their cart.

'Suppose I should move too,' thought Callum.

But the sun was warm and he closed his eyes for a last few seconds, forgetting the past, not worrying about the future, revelling in the tranquillity of the moment. Then, with a sigh, he sat up.

That's when he saw Eli.

It was an easy mistake to make. The man walking towards them was tall, dark and carried himself with a certain authority. But instead of a rod that rested on his shoulder, it was a rifle.

Callum stood up, watching the stranger approach. The children had stopped chattering, Erin was poised motionless, reins in hand, Anna alongside. Even the horses, ears pricked forward, seemed to be listening.

The man stopped at about ten paces. He was probably white, under the dirt; Callum could see small patches of pale skin speckled across his cheeks and neck, like a thrush. His hair was a matted brown rug hanging in tendrils around his ears, dripping down to scrawny shoulders. A filthy grey tee shirt and jeans flapped about his body as he moved. His eyes flickered over the wagon, lingering on the boxes and sacks of food as he inched open his mouth and ran his tongue over his lips. The sunlight glinted on the rifle barrel and made Callum squint.

He pushed back his shoulders, rooting his feet. He wanted to give nothing, to look large. The man dragged his eyes from Callum's wagon and settled on him, then slid over to the women and children. He smirked.

'Moving on are you?'

Callum paused before responding, weighing up the risks of giving away information, while not wanting to antagonise the stranger.

'Yeah, heading north with my family.'

The man seemed to turn the words over. He stared without registering any emotion at the children but his eyes rested rather too long on the women. Erin stared back. Her eyes had all the defiance of a warrior queen. The man's gaze slid away and he nodded towards the cart.

'You got food in there?'

'Some, yes.'

'What kind?'

'Fruit and veg mainly. You want some?'

The man looked at Callum with a kind of pity, then he turned on his heels and ambled away. Erin, Anna and the children didn't move. Callum stayed where he was. He didn't want to break the spell.

The road curved round a huge oak tree and started to dip away south. When he reached the bend the man stopped and turned. Callum had been holding his breath and, without taking his eyes off the figure, opened his mouth and refilled his lungs. The air was warm and still. The man raised his hand. It looked like farewell and, in a way, it was.

****** ****** ******

When Erin tried to remember the murder all she could see in her nightmares were crows.

They weren't real crows, but flapping over sized black shapeless creatures scrabbling over the wagon, the road, Callum, brandishing knives like sharp beaks glinting in the sunshine.

She was familiar with the way scavengers tore at carrion. The crows' of her nightmares had heads that dipped into Callum's warm flesh, spilling its bloodied, yielding, sacred fragility before her disbelieving stare. Shoving and jostling for clear sight. Picking over the remains for scraps of potential nourishment, anything they could take back to feed their own.

If she closed her eyes she shut out the sight of them, but not their sound. Screeching and squawking, panting and screaming. It was a while before she realised the screaming was not the crows but her. The attackers had swooped down, the man's waving arm signalling the arrival of their murdering. Callum had no time to say goodbye, but he'd never stopped acting as a father.

'Erin, save the children!'

He'd bellowed the words before any of them had realised what was happening. She remembered three figures in the attack. The fourth was the man who'd first spoken to them. He was clambering up the side of their cart and, before they could stop him, had Seb by the arm, dragging him towards the edge. Anna was on her feet pulling her son back inside in a slow motion tug of war. The man was winning.

That was when Lucy screamed.

The cart jolted forward and the man lost his balance, spiralling through the air, arms and legs jangling like some crazed puppet. He skidded in the dirt, coming to a halt against a heap of stones, hitting his head hard. He went still. Anna and Seb tumbled backwards and with Lucy fell and bounced against the hard wooden floor. The cart cannoned forward, horses whipped to a gallop by Erin who yahhed them on, slapping the reins leather on leather till dust and sweat mingled and spilt down their sides.

Everyone in the back flayed about, reaching and grabbing, trying to gain a handhold but ricocheting from one side to another, turning somersaults, crashing into each other again and again, thrown into the air as the horses tore the cart through the dips and distortions of the road.

Lucy had managed to wedge herself under the seat, turning her head into the woodwork to try to stop Seb's feet from clipping and scraping her face. It felt an eternity, before the pace slowed, the wind dropped around her and they all landed in a tangled heap. Pushing Seb's legs off her chest she tried to sit and could feel something wet on her face as she wiped her fingers across her mouth. They came back smudged dark red. She wanted to cry, but for some reason neither the sound nor the tears would come.

Suddenly she was smothered by the hot warmth of her mother. Erin had leapt from the seat to grab her. She was shaking and crying, checking Lucy, patting her face, hugging and kissing her, pulling Seb and then Anna close. They clung together, crouched down in the cart.

Lucy managed to wriggle her arms free and wrapped them round her mother's neck, sobbing.

'I want my daddy!'

She squirmed away and half climbed, half fell from the cart, running a few yards before she was grabbed from behind and her mother lifted her off the ground, kicking and screaming. Erin used her weight to pin her down as she fought and struggled to escape.

Anna ran to join them, dragging Seb, gripping his hand.

Erin, half blinded by tears, gathered up Anna and the children, herded them into the cart, urged the ponies onto the path and, glancing behind only for a moment shook the reins together and covered the remaining miles to the island without stopping.

******   ******   ******

The rhythm of the horses' movement rocked them from side to side. After a while Lucy rested her head against Anna who was sat between the children with one arm around each of them. No one spoke.

As the afternoon wore on Lucy and Seb slipped into a deep sleep. It was with a start that they woke to the sound of the steady clopping of hooves.

Lucy had been curled on the floor of the cart, covered by a thin blanket. Seb, who was lying next to her, also stirred. After a moment Lucy began to tremble.

'Mum!'

Erin had her in her arms in an instant, sliding down from the seat at the front and dropping the reins.

'It's alright, sweetheart, I'm here.'

Seb had started to cry. All four of them sat wrapped together, trying to shut out the horror in the comfort of each other's love. They could hear the waves rolling again and again over the shingle. Whenever Erin tried to recall that moment those sounds would always come back to her. Like Lucy, she had wanted her mum, but at the same time she had been thankful Kirsty and Stephen were not with them.

By the time they made their way across the causeway to the island night had fallen.

The waters had drawn back like a curtain, revealing a puddled path shimmering in the moonlight. The air was full of the smell of dank salty seaweed. They were soon across, the way marked by poles driven into the sand on either side, tall enough to poke above the high water mark when the tide was in.

They reached the beach on the other side and were met by the island's Chief Steward.

Erin fell to her knees and wept unashamedly in front of this stranger. Jude knelt beside her and spoke in hushed, soothing tones till she quietened. They were guided through a crowd of around forty people. Lucy and Seb had never seen so many in one place and they clutched their mothers' hands as they climbed trembling from the cart.

They were introduced to a young woman named Karen and spent their first night in her cottage. She gave them warm soup and placed a haphazard set of cushions and mattresses on the floor so they could bed down together in front of the dying embers of a fire. As she closed her eyes Erin always thought she remembered hearing Callum's voice, wishing her sweet dreams and willing her to survive.

******   ******   ******

In the morning there was still no sign of Stephen and Kirsty. After a simple breakfast, Karen took all four of them to Jude's house. It stood in the centre of the village, set a little apart from the others. Erin lifted and dropped the heavy ancient knocker on the front door and the sound echoed around the inside. It opened straightaway and they were ushered in.

Lucy blinked as her eyes adjusted to the darkness. She and Seb were told to sit on the floor and be quiet, something they both found difficult. Erin and Anna looked around registering the simple austerity of the place. A few basic pieces of furniture, a table covered in papers, some books on shelves and no decorations on the whitewashed walls.

Lucy started to cry. Erin picked her up, rocking till the sobs slowed. A hush fell over the cottage.

After a few moments Jude broke the silence.

'All of you are very welcome, including your parents when they arrive. We will do whatever we can to ease your burdens. I hope that you will find healing here and that, one day, we in this Community shall become like a family to you.'

Erin and Anna both looked relieved. 'We will all work hard,' said Anna. 'We understand that we come with very little. Most of what we brought was in the wagon that we had to leave behind. We are entitled to nothing, but we don't ask for charity.'

Jude smiled and his eyes rested on each of them, lingering the longest on the children.

'You bring more than you think.'

'In what way?'

He sighed. 'We face deep challenges here. Some years ago our Community divided with a few of our number heading even further north, believing that they had more hope of survival in a place that offered greater diversity. My father and I stayed but he died, leaving me with a responsibility to bear for those left behind, many of whom are now too weak to work.

'This stewardship is a heavy burden that I carry. Over the years we have encountered others like yourselves making a similar search for a new beginning. Some have stayed, content with our simple life and grateful for what we can offer, some have made the decision to keep going. I suspect that you will be no different.'

A look passed between Erin and Anna. Seb had crawled into Anna's lap, his thumb in his mouth, face tear streaked. All their eyes rested on Jude. Erin spoke for them all.

'We won't be leaving, Jude.'

She looked at Anna who nodded and making her excuses hurried the children from the cottage.

'Come on you two, let's go and see what we can find to do outside.'

When they were gone, Erin turned to Jude.

'Lucy and Seb can't know the truth about what's happened to Callum.'

'I understand. You want the children to believe in grownups as bigger, stronger, more powerful; people they can depend on to keep nightmares at bay, to protect them with a strong shield that's always there, keeping them safe. If that's what you want then we can tell them that story. '

And so, from this desire to protect the children, a tale about each of their fathers was born. One told so often that, over the years, even the adults almost came to believe it was true. Seb's father, Eli, became a hero, who'd died worn out from caring for his family. Lucy's father, Callum, became a man whose heart had been broken from loving them too much.

And in the meantime the crows that lurked deep in all of their memories and held the real truth became buried black shadows, the stuff of nightmares.

December 24th 2085

Erin woke early as usual and lay trying not to move, listening to Lucy's gentle breathing.

As quietly as she could she slid out of the bed she shared with her daughter, placing her feet into sheepskin slippers and wrapping round her the heavy brown coat that doubled as a dressing gown. The bedroom door creaked as it opened and she froze, willing Lucy not to wake. The child stirred, snuffled and then settled back into the warm space left by her mother's body. Erin breathed again. She'd got away with getting up without waking her for once.

Tiptoeing outside into the yard to the toilet she attended to this first priority. Then, back indoors, she turned her energies to the next task. With great care, she began to feed the dying embers of the fire in the grate to inject warmth and light into the room.

The dry twigs caught and crackled into life and Erin sat back on her heels, taking a moment to enjoy their warmth. Then Lucy wailed and, sighing, her day began in earnest.

'Hello darling,' she murmured.

Tousle haired, Lucy was sitting up in bed, with the crumpled look of early morning. The room was still dark and Erin slipped back under the covers, smoothing Lucy's hair from her eyes and depositing kisses on her nose. The child squirmed and screwed her eyes up tight.

'Ooh, grumpy face this morning.'

They lay with their heads alongside each other, Erin gathering her thoughts. She ran one finger along Lucy's cheek, its smooth softness warm and perfect to her touch.

'Do you know what's special about today Lucy?'

There was the briefest of pauses and then the child squealed: 'Presents!'

Erin hugged her tight, tickling her face with her hair and making her giggle. 'If we could bottle that laugh we'd make a fortune,' they had often said. It was the sound a parent would never tire of hearing.

'Not today silly, but tomorrow, if we've been really good, we'll all get presents.'

Christmas was a time for tradition and she and Anna had discovered that it was no different in this Community. Lots of people had shared knowledge to help them to settle in, but their main source of information was Izzie.

They'd met Izzie on their first morning shortly after they'd spoken to Jude. She'd been on her way to the cottage in the centre of the village that the Community used for its nursery and school. Her job was to make sure the children were safe and cared for. In spite of her efforts there were fewer children joining the Community each year, but as they got to know her better Erin and Anna could not imagine anyone more perfect for the role.

She had stopped in her tracks when she saw the four of them emerging from Jude's cottage.'

'Well, good morning to you. And what might you be calling your wee selves might I ask?'

The children had each taken a step closer to their mothers. Lucy's thumb went to her mouth and Seb turned into Anna's skirts.

'Say hello Lucy.'

The thumb remained where it was.

'So it's Lucy is it? That's a lovely name. One of my favourites as it happens. Mine's Izzy. Can you say that?'

'Izzy.'

'That's really good. Izzy. And what's this lovely lad called?'

Seb turned and looked over his shoulder, appearing fascinated by Izzy's footwear. It wasn't every day you saw an apple shaped woman in contrasting coloured wellingtons.

'This is Seb,' said Anna. 'He doesn't feel like talking today.'

'Well of course, this'll all take a bit of getting used to I expect. Do you like my boots, Seb? Know what colour they are?'

Lucy's thumb was out.

'Yellow!'

All three women laughed.

'Clever girl. Yes, this one's yellow, but this other one's red. I couldn't find two the same colour and anyway, this might start a new fashion. What do you reckon?'

The children gave their mothers a look that said 'Who is this crazy person?' She wasn't like any of the grownups they'd met in their lives so far. But they liked her.

Erin found her voice. 'Sorry, I'm Erin, and this is my sister, Anna. We arrived last night.'

Izzy paused. 'I heard what happened. Devastating, absolutely devastating.'

Erin tightened her grip on Lucy's hand without being aware of what she was doing. Feeling Anna's arm circling her waist she fought back the tears that threatened to burst out and overwhelm her. She didn't want to cry in front of the children.

No one spoke for a few minutes. Then Lucy broke the silence.

'Baabaas!'

Everyone turned in the direction the little girl was pointing. Sure enough, coming round the side of the cottages and into the lane was a small flock of sheep herded by a young man and a black and white collie. The dog scurried back and forth, never taking its eyes off the animals, attentive to their every move.

'Morning Tom,' called Izzy. 'This is Lucy and Seb, Anna and Erin. They've just arrived last night.'

The lad raised his cap and waved to them.

'Hi. Sorry I can't stop. Catch you this evening at the Gathering House.' He disappeared round the corner, running to keep up with the livestock, whistling to the dog.

'Bye bye baabaas,' waved Lucy.

'So you like animals do you Lucy? Would you and Seb like to come to my house and see some more? And maybe your mums would like some breakfast?'

She turned to Erin and Anna. 'We've got a cottage that we use for the children to come to while their parents are working. It's a sort of nursery. We all take turns to help out, but I'm the one in charge. And that' she laughed as she crouched down to Lucy and Seb's height 'is because I'm Mrs Bossy Boots.'

They followed Izzy and a few minutes later reached a dwelling larger than most of the others in the village. A wooden fence ran round a cottage garden filled with an assortment of different flowers, fruits, vegetables and, it had to be said, a lot of weeds. The fence was decorated with shells and pebbles, feathers and leaves tucked under posts, pushed into knot holes or wedged between planks.

Izzy untied the piece of old rope knotted round the gate and half lifting it on its rusty hinges pushed it open and ushered them through.

'Lucy, Seb, this is where I come every day to play. You can come too if you want.'

Inside the rooms held a wild assortment of objects gathered from the fields and shore. Through the window Erin could see that some had been crafted into an obstacle course of planks, swings and seesaws that a small group of children, some around Lucy and Seb's age, some older, were clambering over. Wild flowers and dried leaves festooned window ledges, planted in a jumble of containers:

chipped cups, old jars, hollowed out tree trunks. Two of the children were rummaging through a basket of hats, gloves, ribbons, shoes and scarves.

'You two having fun?' asked Izzy. 'This is Seb and Lucy. They're going to be our new friends. I bet they'd like to make some noise. Can you show them where the drums are?'

The children soon found themselves the centre of attention with two other women joining them on the floor and showing them how to play the drum. Izzy nudged Erin and Anna.

'They seem happy enough. Time for a chat?'

She led them through to the kitchen where a little boy was standing on a stool at the sink, a look of intense concentration on his face as he sailed a folded paper boat up and down the water.

'That's going to sink soon Billy. You might want to go and find something that'll float better than paper.'

He carried on, lost in his imagination until the boat did finally become saturated and he clambered down and onto Izzy's lap. She handed him what looked like a recently baked biscuit which he crammed into his mouth, fingers splaying across his face as he chewed and swallowed.

'Right, that's you sorted. Go and play outside now. And don't forget your coat.'

Handing around steaming cups of mint tea to Anna and Erin, Izzy settled with a sigh into an ancient rocking chair. Somewhere a clock ticked. Nothing was said. They each sipped at their tea till it was gone, allowing its warmth to soothe them. And then Erin stood up.

'We'd better see to the children.'

'Of course dear, I understand.'

They made sure Lucy and Seb were wrapped up warm and said their goodbyes. When they got to the door Izzy hugged each of them.

'I want you girls to know that we are all here for you. We'll do anything we can to help. Jude'll be round to see you again later to get you sorted with a proper roof over your heads. But call in here whenever you feel like it. You're always welcome.'

Both sisters murmured a thank you.

'We all have stories to tell on this island. Not all are like yours of course, but they are stories nonetheless. It's those stories that bind us together. When you're ready, you can tell us yours.

December 2085

December 25th dawned bleak and frosty, everywhere blasted by a moaning wind that rattled tiles and threatened to blow in windows.

'Lucy's got a temperature,' Erin announced opening the door to Anna's knock, a wriggling bundle wailing in her arms. 'She won't settle. I've been up and down all night.'

She looked exhausted.

'Give her here,' said Anna. 'Happy Christmas eh!'

It wasn't going to be easy. Family rituals at such times never were. Empty chairs cried out, memories came flooding back.

'Keep going. You have to,' Erin had said to herself as she'd nursed Lucy. Heat radiated from her daughter's small body and she'd stripped off her clothes and was bathing her forehead.

'Please don't be poorly Lucy,' she'd whispered. 'Mummy loves you so much.'

Callum had always loved Christmas. She tried not to think about the past. That life had gone. They had to look to the future, if only for the children's sake.

Deciding against battling the elements to get to the gathering planned in the church, they instead put extra logs on the fire and hunkered down for the day. When Erin peered round the curtains she saw grey mist shrouding the island into monochrome colours. Skeletal trees stretched their fleshless fingers into the sky. Even the holly bush berries looked black, lustreless leaves twisted into thorny daggers.

'Let's eat.' They did their best with what they had but, in the end, it was too hard to pretend that this was a happy Christmas and they survived the day in a daze of sadness. Lucy slept till late afternoon, and when she woke her temperature had gone down and she seemed a little better. She smiled up at her mother and nibbled at some bread. Erin knelt at her side and kissed her cheek. That smile was all the Christmas present she wanted.

By about four o'clock it was starting to get dark so they were surprised when there was a knock at the door and Jude arrived. He shook off the rain from his thick coat and stamped his feet on the rug at the door.

'We missed you this morning.'

Seb and Lucy continued to play at Anna's feet.

'I'm sorry. We'd have come but Lucy wasn't too well and...' Erin's voice trailed away.

Jude rested his eyes on Erin. For a moment she thought she might lose control and cry again. She gulped and looked away.

He stayed for a short while, carefully checking they were all safe, had what they needed. Jude was always formal, focused and full of intent. What the visit might have lacked in warmth it made up for in practicalities.

When he'd gone Erin drew the thick curtains over the doors and windows, turning the cottage into a cave filled with shadows from the fire that danced on walls and ceiling. The children each snuggled into their mothers, thumbs in their mouths, eyes growing heavy in the darkness.

Anna sighed. 'I suppose we should be grateful.'

Erin nodded. Each cottage had an allotment though the timing of their arrival meant they had relied on the generosity of others for food at first. In return they had offered their skills. They had shared recipes for remedies from plants and herbs handed down through generations.

It hadn't taken long for Lucy and Seb to settle. They sometimes stopped their play on the shoreline and stood hand in hand, staring towards the horizon as if watching for someone coming. Erin found she could distract Lucy, unless she was tired or fractious. Then she would become furious with impotent rage, pummelling her mother with tiny fists, 'Why no daddy?'

She woke screaming most nights for the first few months. Those terrors gradually diminished. Erin found that sharing her bed helped Lucy to settle.

'To be honest, having her close is a comfort.' she'd explained to Anna.

She knew that after what had happened to Eli at the hands of murderers, no one would understand that need to be held more than her sister.

June 2086

As time passed, life fell into a new rhythm.

'Sometimes I find I haven't given Callum a thought for hours,' Erin said to Anna. 'I feel so guilty.'

'Don't be,' said Anna. 'It's normal. It doesn't mean you love Callum any less or that you've forgotten him, any more than I've forgotten Eli. We have to move on or we'd go mad.'

Erin knew she was right, but that didn't make it any easier.

Each day they woke early, left the children with Izzie and then made a start on whatever tasks the Community, under Jude's stewardship, had prioritised for them. It soon became apparent that the island could carry no passengers.

'This way of living suits some more than others,' Jude had explained. 'We have people that stay for a while and then go elsewhere. They feel they want to be independent. Or they realise they can't contribute enough to justify their place here. On the whole we're left to get on with our lives and make the best of the hand we've been dealt.'

Erin and Anna found it suited them.

'The nursery means we can work, Lucy and Seb are thriving,' said Erin. 'They're making friends with the other children, and I feel part of a community.'

She wanted to know about the history of the place and spoke to Jude about it. He was only too willing to share the story with her.

'Some of the people that live here have family connections stretching back years,' he explained. 'Others are newcomers who feel there's nothing to be gained from engaging with the outside world and they fear it. They've had enough of its dramas and disasters and are glad to make a fresh start, embracing a more basic way of life.'

'Life here's not perfect, Erin, as you can see. It's got its challenges like everywhere else. We each have to weigh up the choices and make the decisions about our responsibilities to this Community. We have to decide what's fair, what's right.'

'You said you had family here once. Where did they go?'

'Most of my family moved north. My father put a different value from them on caring for those that could no longer care for themselves. In the end, he felt how we deal with the vulnerable came down to practicalities, for my uncle and aunt it was about compassion.'

'My father thought my uncle's views too simplistic. He felt we should have seen this tension around resources to keep us alive coming,' Jude continued. 'I am not a parent myself, Erin. But I too have stories of loss in my family. My grandparents' youngest child was called Mia. When still a baby, like so many others she became ill. They would have done anything to save her. But they couldn't; the drugs that might have helped her were rationed and she didn't fit the criteria. You could say the system, not her parents, failed and that perhaps it's carried on doing so.'

'So do you think people that can't work because they're too old or sick should offer up their lives as a sacrifice?' Erin asked.

'Any such offering is for the good of the whole Community. I prefer to call it a gift. After all, there is no greater love than that of a man who lays down his life for his friends.'

Erin turned these words over for a few days before telling Anna. She was speechless.

'That's pretty brutal.'

'Maybe. But what choices do we have?'

'Are you sure this is a choice?'

'I think Jude's suggesting it is.'

Anna was quiet

'Perhaps, but if it comes across as an expectation then it could become very hard to swim against that tide.'

'I know,' said Erin. 'Izzie was telling me about an old couple the other day that used to live in our cottage. One day they walked out into the sea and didn't come back. Their names are on a plaque in the church.'

Erin thought about these conversations as she lay in bed that night listening to Lucy's steady breathing. Names on a plaque, words in a song, faces in a photograph. In the end they were all just stories, chalk lines on concrete that could be washed away by the rain. Did any of it matter, as long as they did no harm?

Two Years Later

August 2088

Erin winced as she rested her hands on her back and straightened up. She wasn't sure how much more of this she could take today.

The sun had been blistering, sapping all of their energies when there was so much to do.

'You OK?' Anna tipped a bucket load of fruit into the crate and flopped down next to her. 'You look all in.'

'It's the heat. I've not known it this bad before.'

Anna was worried. It was hot, there was no denying that. But her sister hadn't looked well for a while. She'd lost weight, her skin and hair seemed lustreless and she'd had frequent episodes of overwhelming fatigue.

'How are you sleeping?'

'Fine, don't worry about me. I'm just a bit run down that's all. Now, what's next on the list?'

******   ******   ******

As time went on it became more and more apparent that Erin was not well.

'I can't seem to concentrate,' she moaned to Anna. 'And I keep getting this tingling in my hands. And look at my hair! I'm scared to brush it in case any more falls out.'

Anna bit her lip. Other people were starting to notice, she'd had two or three people ask her if Erin was alright and she was running out of excuses to cover for her.

Lucy and Seb also seemed to have picked up on the changes in Erin. Anna encouraged Lucy to come across to her cottage to play as much as she could in an attempt to give her sister a chance to rest. But she'd noticed that they both turned to her when they needed something, as if they sensed Erin's fatigue.

'What do you think's making you feel like this? You're not yourself.'

'I don't know. Some days I feel fine, others I don't know how I get out of bed.'

'Does anything hurt?'

'When it's bad, everything hurts, my joints, my muscles. And I'm always so thirsty.'

They didn't need to say anything more. Whatever was wrong with Erin, this was bad.

****** ****** ******

Jude called one evening. Anna was sorting through the children's clothes, setting some aside for mending and putting those they'd grown out of into a pile to take to Izzie for others to have. Erin was in a chair at the window, attempting to sew but struggling to focus. Her eyes felt tired, she'd woken that morning with double vision and she'd had to rest all day, till they settled back to normal.

'I will take some water, thank you,' said Jude in response to Anna's enquiry. 'I won't stay long, I am sure you are both weary.'

Anna brought across three cups. Erin drank from hers and poured a second before the others had even started. Jude studied her.

'We missed you today, Erin.'

His tone was calm, soft. It invited the listener to share confidences. Anna shifted in her chair.

'I think she's picked up some sort of virus,' she said. 'She'll be fine.'

Jude acknowledged this with a slow nod, keeping his eyes fixed on Erin. She said nothing and continued to stare out of the window.

'And you Erin, what do you think? Is it a virus you have?'

'I don't know, maybe. I don't feel well sometimes. It comes and goes'

'Sometimes? So this has happened before?'

Erin nodded.

'Can we help you? Are there tasks we can give to others till you feel better? Would you like to try a potion?'

Anna cut in.

'Thanks Jude, but we're managing between us. I can look after Lucy, she and Seb are no bother and they both help out. We'll be fine.'

He smiled. 'I understand. You want to be independent, deal with this as a family. But you have a Community around you now. And we care for our own.'

Reaching into his pocket, Jude slipped a small notebook across the table.

'Perhaps it would help if you kept a record of your symptoms Erin?'

They all looked at the notebook until, with a sigh, Erin picked it up.

'I'm always telling Lucy to write stories,' she said. 'I suppose there's no reason why I shouldn't as well.'

Jude stood up.

'We are all stories in the end, Erin. Some people think they're already written before we're even born, but I prefer to believe we write our own. Perhaps think how you can make yours a good one.'

August 2093

Dear Jude, Is there any more news on Erin? Hope

Dear Hope, I am concerned for her welfare, of course, but we cannot carry on like this for ever. I have the Community as a whole to think about. Jude

But Jude, she has a child!

Even more reason not to be so selfish. That child has family.

How old is Lucy now?

Eleven.

You can't expect a mother to leave an eleven year old.

You make it sound like she's an asset to her daughter, Hope, and she's not. As she has grown more ill she has become a burden.

Her family are never going to see it like that.

Perhaps not, but Erin will.

Because, Jude, you're making her feel she should.

On the contrary, I have merely given her the facts as I see them.

Which are?

Lots of children are orphans. Not all parents are good for children.

Jude, I know you didn't have the best of relationships with yours, but that doesn't mean children don't need parents.

Erin doesn't just have Lucy's welfare to consider. She's got to think about how her behaviour impacts on the rest of the Community.

Why?

Because that's her duty, and Erin knows this only too well.

Love is more important than duty, Jude. Lucy and her mother will value any time they have together.

Of course. Erin's death is not imminent. We want her to live as long as is practicable. But I am not permitted to be ruled by my heart.

Why not?

Because as Chief Steward in this Community I have to use my head.

Two Years Later

August 2095

My Story: by Lucy Daniel

I was born in 2082 which makes me 13 years old. So far I have lived in three different places in my life.

The first two we had to leave because they weren't safe anymore. A long time ago we moved to this third one which is a cottage on a sort of island. I say 'sort of' because when the tide is low you can just walk off, you don't need a boat. All you have to do is go across a kind of sandbank to the mainland. I've done that a few times, but mostly I stay here.

My mum and I moved here when I was about two. We came with my aunt and cousin. They are called Anna and Seb and live next door. Seb's not only my cousin; he's also my best friend. My grandparents came too.

Mum told me that when I was little my dad died of a heart attack. I can't really remember him, but she put a photo of them both on the window sill in our cottage so I know what he looked like. On the way here she says some strangers stole the food we had in our wagon. I used to have nightmares about it. I don't any more, but I still feel scared when I see big black birds because my nightmares were always about huge crows that swooped down and tried to hurt me. I couldn't get away from them and they pecked and pecked till I was dead.

Sometimes I feel really sad and I don't know why. Partly that's why I'm writing this story. Mum likes writing. She says writing things down helps her get things straight. You don't have to show anyone what you've written if you don't want to.

I'm not sure what I'm going to do with this story when I've finished. I might let Seb see it, but I haven't decided. He's a boy and he doesn't always understand why writing things down and talking about stuff is important.

When I was born we lived in a lighthouse. I wish I could remember that. It's still there, about a day's ride away, and sometimes new people arrive here who have been to it. Seb's dad was called Eli and he used to go fishing from the lighthouse. He was really good and everyone was jealous of him because he always caught more than anyone else.

The second place we lived was with our grandparents. Seb and I haven't seen them for a long time and it's really hard to find out how they are because they decided they needed too much looking after here and went off in Grandad's boat to find somewhere new to live. I think Mum misses them a lot, I know I do. Grandad used to teach me how to play the ukulele and Gran let me cook with her and told me what it was like when she and Grandpa were young and there were lots of things to do that we don't have any more.

Sometimes when Mum's told me stories about them she gets sad. She tries not to show it but I can tell. We don't even know if they're alive. If they are they'll be ever so old and probably won't be able to do much, which is why I think Mum worries about them. Seb thinks they might be dead and, if they are it wouldn't be so bad, as long as they're together. I don't know how I feel about that because I liked having them live on the island with us. But if they did need a lot of looking after they couldn't live with us anyway, even if they wanted to and even though they're family. I didn't use to understand why that was, because families usually do want to be together. But Mum always says they didn't want to live with us and be a burden and that's what the Community here would say they were and they'd hate that.

Mum has a silver necklace with an oak tree on it that Gran gave to her. It's been in the family a long time so when she gives it to me I'll always keep it safe. One day I might be able to give it to my little girl, if I ever have one.

Everyone in the Community here works hard. We have to because otherwise we wouldn't have enough to eat. Sometimes the weather's really bad and we don't have a good harvest. If people are sick or old, can't work and need looking after it's a big problem for us.

That's what Mum meant about not being a burden.

When I was six Mum started to feel ill. At first she just got tired all the time. She wasn't that old so we all just thought she'd get better if she took things a bit easier. Jude used to come round most days to see how she was feeling. He always asked her loads of questions and wrote all her answers down in his notebook. I used to wonder if he was planning to write a story about her one day, like I'm doing.

Jude's not a doctor or anything; he's what's called the Chief Steward of our Community. That means he has a lot of responsibility. He helped when we first got here, made sure we had somewhere to live and that Mum and Anna had help with looking after me and Seb so they could work for the Community.

Jude doesn't have any children or family of his own which means he has more time to look after others. Or at least, that's what Mum says. She says she feels a bit sorry for him because he lives alone and hasn't really got any friends. I don't know what happened to his family, but his parents are dead and I think they didn't get on too well anyway. He told me once he has a cousin like I do, but she lives somewhere else now and so he doesn't see her anymore. She's called Hope, which I think is a really nice name.

Jude spends a lot of time with old and sick people, like Mum. There's not much he can do to help them, the only medicines we have are things we can make from herbs and plants and Jude knows a lot about those, what's good for you and what's poisonous, and makes up potions that people can take if they want or he says it'll help them.

When people are very sick Jude sits with them and talks to them a lot and sometimes he even takes them into his cottage. When they die he organises for them to be buried. There's a church on the island with a big churchyard and most people end up there. I sometimes wonder if that's what'll happen to me when I've had my turn of being alive.

Mum being ill has made a big difference to my life. I try helping her, but what I really want is for her to be well again. I worry about how we're going to look after her and why it should be her and not someone else that's already really old that's got sick.

It's not fair.

It's worse when I'm tired or if I haven't slept much. That happens quite a lot when I'm worrying about her. Sometimes I get really bad tummy aches. Then I go for a long walk with my dog, Lela, but I don't always have the time for that either. I can talk to my Auntie Anna, but mostly I try to keep things to myself, she's got a lot to worry about too with taking care of all of us.

I did try talking to Jude once. He asked me how much time it took looking after Mum and said I was a good girl for helping, but that I shouldn't forget there were lots of other things that I needed to learn about and that Mum wouldn't want me to feel like she was a burden to me or any of the rest of the Community. I felt a bit confused and tried to explain that she was my mum and I loved her very much. So even though I didn't like her being ill, and got tired sometimes, I didn't want to stop looking after her, I just wanted her to get better.

Jude said sometimes when people got ill they could be a bit selfish and had I ever thought about that. I said I didn't think it was selfish if you couldn't help it, but he said sometimes people decided they'd had their turn and it wasn't fair to carry on and expect other people to look after you.

That's when I thought about my grandparents and knew no matter how much I wanted to I wasn't ever going to see them again after all. And that made me feel really sad and I wondered if they had missed me the way I missed them.

I asked Mum about it and she said me and Seb had been really special to Gran and Gramps. Though she understood why I would have liked to still have them live here and it was hard for me to understand, them not staying with us to the island when they were too old to help out was the best way they had of showing that they loved us.

I asked if that's what Jude meant about not being selfish and everyone having a turn. She gave me a hug and said she loved me more than anything in the world and that the most important thing in life was to make things a little bit better for people you loved if you could and to do no one any harm.

So that's what I've decided I'm going to try my very best to do from now on.

The End

If you want to know what happens to Lucy, here's a taster from the next book in the series:

20/20 Vision: They didn't see it coming

One life, two questions:

What's fair?

What's right?

When you live in a Community with barely enough resources to go round you ask those questions every day. Is it fair that some people don't work? Is it right to keep feeding someone that's never going to get better?

But what if you love that person more than anyone else in the world? Lucy Daniel has struggled with these questions her whole life. It's 2099 and global disasters have changed everything. It means there's no room for sentiment.

Jude's in charge. He says her Mum's sacrifice was noble. That's not how it feels to Lucy. And now she has a chance to tell their story and change everything. But will Jude allow her to speak?

A book for anyone that's wondered if it's ever enough just to say 'I care.'

Available from Amazon

https://www.amazon.co.uk/20-Vision-They-didnt-coming/dp/1539045900

Check us out or get in touch through Facebook:

https://www.facebook.com/suemiller2020author/

What the reviews say about
20/20 Vision: They didn't see it coming:

This is an engaging and deeply thought provoking book. The best dystopias present the horrors of the future and force the reader to reflect on the here and now...it reminded me of 'Sophie's World'. The characters are well drawn and the layers of the plot peel away with twists and turns to surprise.

A story that's both frightening and exhilarating at the same time. Can't stop talking to people about it. Beautifully and skilfully written, full of questions and surprising answers.

I was intrigued by the premise of this novel 'What's fair? What's right?' A thought provoking look at our way of life through the lens of a 17 year old in a very different society in 2099

The location is achingly familiar (un-named, but obviously Holy Island!) and the events of a dystopian future which looks back on our current society and the issues facing us now make this a warning as well as a relentlessly good read.

This compelling view of a future following climate change disaster says a lot about human frailty, but even more of the power of compassion and the eternal resilience of the human spirit

24887498R00145

Made in the USA
Columbia, SC
29 August 2018